Alfred M. Heston

Heston's Hand Book of Atlantic City

Seashore sketches - winter and summer attractions - memoranda and ready

reference for visitors.

Alfred M. Heston

Heston's Hand Book of Atlantic City
Seashore sketches - winter and summer attractions - memoranda and ready reference for visitors.

ISBN/EAN: 9783337255718

Printed in Europe, USA, Canada, Australia, Japan

Cover: Foto ©Andreas Hilbeck / pixelio.de

More available books at **www.hansebooks.com**

J. D. SOUTHWICK,
MANAGER

DIRECTLY
ON THE BEACH

The
Shelburne

MICHIGAN
AVENUE

REMAINS OPEN THROUGHOUT THE YEAR. EVERY
CONVENIENCE, INCLUDING HOT AND COLD
SEA WATER BATHS, AND PASSENGER
ELEVATOR.

THE A. B. ROBERTS CO.

The Shelburne

HOTEL TRAYMORE

ON THE OCEAN FRONT

Has Enlarged to Double its Former Capacity

The Traymore has long been recognized as one of Atlantic City's most popular and famous beach front hotels; and the extensive alterations and additions just completed make it a model of comfort and elegance.

Rooms en Suite, Baths attached, Etc., Etc.

CAPACITY, 400   **D. S. WHITE, Jr., Owner and Proprietor**

THE NEW HOTEL LURAY

Entirely Rebuilt, with Large Rooms, Single and En Suite, with Private Sea and Fresh Water Baths

Piazza joined to the Boardwalk. Heated Sun Parlor and Pavilion on the Ocean

Write for Illustrated Booklet to   **JOSIAH WHITE & SON**   Open every month in the Year

17

HOTEL ST. CHARLES

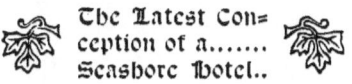 The Latest Con=
ception of a.......
Seashore Hotel..

Directly on the Ocean Front, at the foot of St. Charles Place, Two
Hundred feet from the Breakers.

Most Artistic Building in Atlantic City.

Thoroughly Modern in all its Appointments.

Forty Rooms En Suite with Private Bath.

An ever-flowing artesian well on the premises, bringing the water
crystal pure, from a depth of 1000 feet. Ball and music
room, 60 x 75 feet, large dining room, seating
500. Reception Halls, etc.

See view opposite page 52.   James B. Reilly.

Seaside House
ATLANTIC CITY.

Pennsylvania
Avenue,
Ocean Front

Overlooking the Ocean
Enlarged and Refurnished throughout

ACCOMMODATIONS FOR 250 GUESTS.

Sun Gallery. Elevators. Hot and Cold Salt Water Baths in the House.
Enclosed walk of glass from Hotel to Beach. Billiard room and all the
appointments of a first-class house. Coach meets all trains. Ocean parlor on the beach, free to guests. Telegraph and Long Distance Telephone in the house.

CHARLES EVANS.

See view opposite page 92.   Open all the Year.

18

The Rudolf

HOTEL ISLESWORTH

...OPEN ...ALL ...YEAR

VIRGINIA AVENUE,
Directly on the Beach

A Modern Hotel
Twelfth Season under same
Management

FRESH AND SALT WATER IN ALL BATH ROOMS

A. C. McCLELLAN.

See view opposite page 102

ORCHESTRA   **MILITARY BAND**

Rooms en Suite with Sea and Fresh Water
Baths. Elevator from Street Level and complete Electric Plant. Steam Heat. Sun Parlor. A Table d'Hote Luncheon and Dinner
served in Cafe. ·.   ·.   ·.   ·.   ·.

Hotel Rudolf
On Beach Front

Terms, $3.00 to $5.00 per day.
Special Rates for May, June and September.

W. E. COCHRAN,
Chief Clerk.

CHARLES R. MYERS,
Proprietor.

19

..The Wiltshire..

VIRGINIA AVENUE

Seventy-five yards from the Beach and New Steel Pier

An old established hotel, rebuilt and much improved. Every modern convenience. Accommodations for 300 guests. Open from March until October. Rooms en suite, with private bath. Furnished throughout with an eye to the perfection of detail in the matter of bedding, furniture and appointments.

The cuisine will receive the personal attention of the owner and manager, Mr. S. S. Phoebus, formerly connected with the Hygeia, at Old Point Comfort.

For terms and full particulars address

S. S. PHOEBUS
Owner and Proprietor

THE... IROQUOIS

A SUPERB NEW HOTEL

South Carolina Ave. and Beach

Ocean view; capacity 500; steam heat; sun parlors; elevator to street; rooms en suite, with bath; spring rates, $12 to $17.50 weekly; booklet mailed.

W. F. SHAW

—BY THE BREAKERS AT BRIGANTINE—

Holland House

SAFE SURF BATHING

Take Steamer at the Inlet, electric cars to the door
See Brigantine Transportation Company's Advertisement

Opened in 1896. Supplied with Artesian well water Lighted by Electricity
Meals served at any hour à la carte. Fish and Game Dinners a Specialty

EUGENE MEHL, Manager

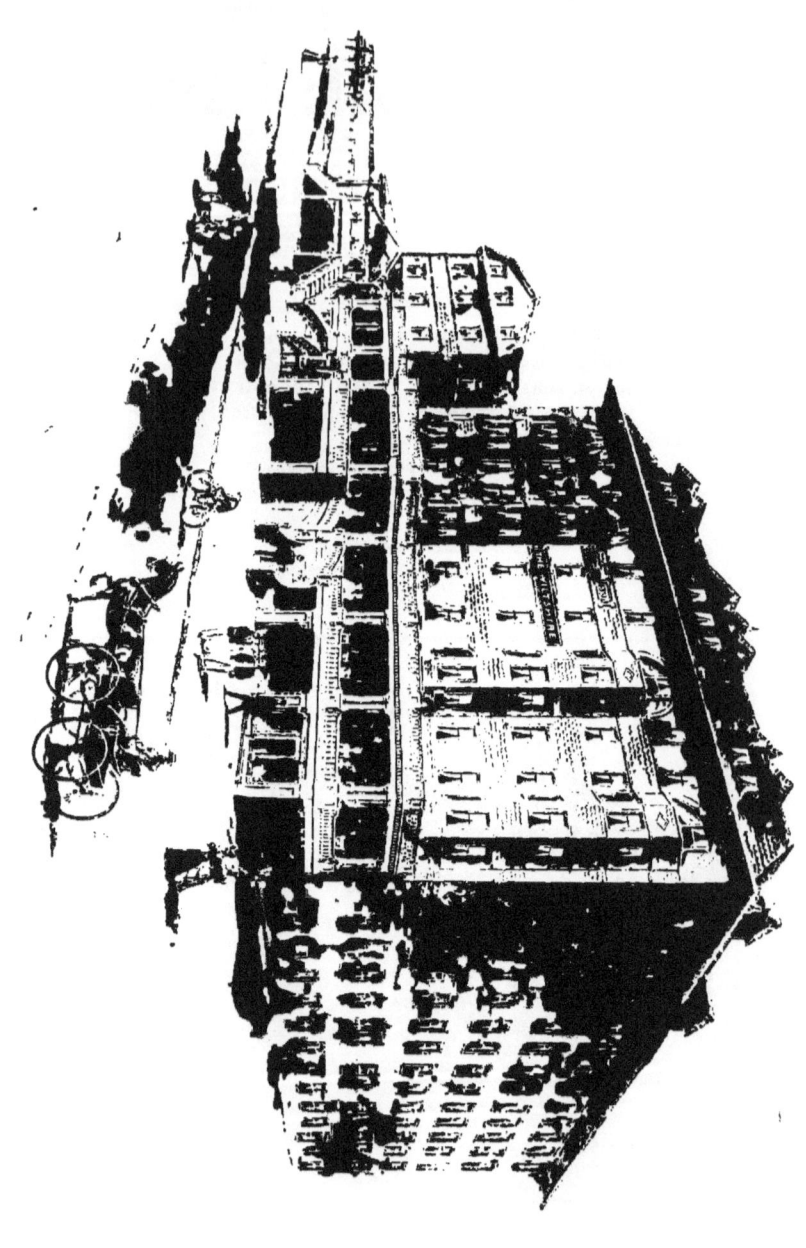

Hotel Atglen

MICHIGAN AVE.
NEAR BEACH

OCEAN VIEW
STEAM HEAT
OPEN ALL THE YEAR

Strictly first-class family House. All modern improvements. Special rates to families. $8.00 to $10.00 a week, $1.50 to $2.00 per day.

J. E. REED

THE ROMAN

Ocean End   St. Charles Place

European and American. Meals served to order from 6 A. M. until 12 M. at night. New and elaborately furnished in ancient and modern designs. Rooms en suite or single, with bath. Elevator to street level.

OPEN ALL THE YEAR   **A. B. ALEXANDER**

THE LAMARTINE

Corner Connecticut and Oriental Avenues

$1.50 TO $2.50 PER DAY
SPECIAL RATES BY THE WEEK   **MOORE & MIDDLETON**

CUISINE THE BEST   OPEN ALL THE YEAR   EXCELLENT
STEAM HEAT   ACCOMMODATION

THE BERWICK

JNO. M. TAYLOR   **KENTUCKY AVENUE**
PROPRIETOR   ½-Square from Beach

THE HOWARD

TENNESSEE AVENUE
Near the Beach

M. SCHNEIDER

$2.00 to $2.50 per day $8.00 to $14.00 per week

Hotel Majestic

VIRGINIA AVE., THIRD HOUSE FROM THE BEACH
Directly overlooking the New Steel Pier
Entirely new management and service

Elevator. Modern in every detail. Capacity 300
Booklet mailed on application

SAM'L C. OSBORNE
OSCAR D. PAINTER

21

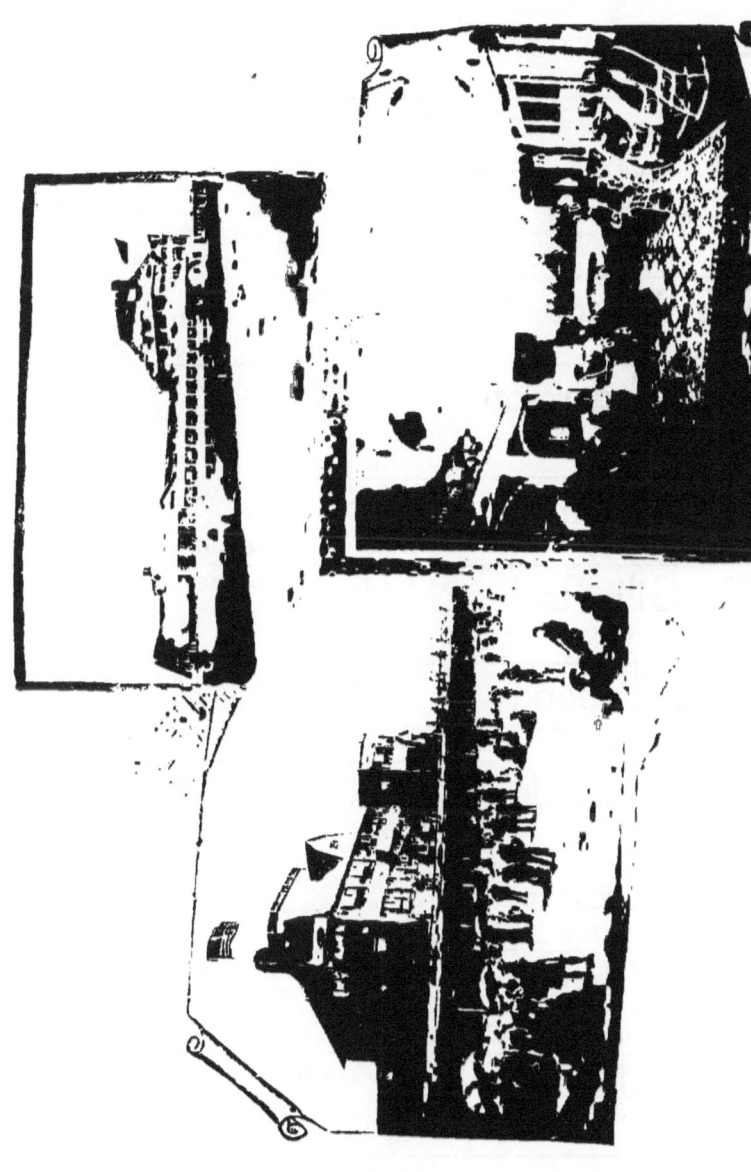

Atlantic City Casino—Interior and Exterior Views

Hotel Stickney

KENTUCKY AVE.   100 FT. FROM THE CCEAN

L. V. STICKNEY

Steam Heat. Elevator. $9.00 to $14.00 per week   Transient, $2.00 to $2.50 per day

Norwood

KENTUCKY AVE., second house from Beach

F. ALSFELT

Appointments First-class   Steam Heat   Open all the Year   Location very desirable

Hotel Marsden

OCEAN END OF SOUTH CAROLINA AVENUE

L. A. CHARLTON

Newly Furnished   Open all the Year

The Walton

141 OCEAN AVENUE

MRS. THOMAS McLAUGHLIN, Proprietress

Terms Moderate.   Open all the Year

Hotel Cedarcroft

SOUTH CAROLINA AVE. AND BEACH

JOSEPH F. MEGILL, Manager

Formerly of Waverly Hotel, Bedford Springs

Fine Ocean View. Centrally Located. Modern Conveniences. Convenient to Railroad Stations and Places of Interest. Rates: Per day, $2.50 to $3.00. Special Weekly Rates

OPEN ALL THE YEAR

La Belle Inn

SOUTH CAROLINA AVE. Near Beach

MRS. L. H. SOOY

Open all the Year   Remodeled and Refurnished

The Gilberta

154 and 156 OCEAN AVE., near Beach

MRS. S. F. HARRIS

A cheerful family house   Good table   Delightful location   Steam heat

OPEN ALL THE YEAR

Hotel Esmond

OCEAN END NEW YORK AVENUE

P. L. ELWOOD

Brand new and first-class in all respects   Every convenience   Elevator to street level

$2.00 daily, up $10.00 weekly, up   Booklet mailed

The Seaward

1302 PACIFIC AVENUE

Between South Carolina and Tennessee

Excellent Cuisine   With home comforts   MRS. N L. WARD

OPEN ALL THE YEAR

Hotel Heckler

COR. ATLANTIC AND PENNSYLVANIA AVES

HENRY HECKLER, Proprietor

OPEN ALL THE YEAR   Heated by steam in Winter

Hotel Kilcourse

COR. ARCTIC AND ARKANSAS AVENUES

Open all the Year

A brick Hotel, newly furnished   With modern appointments

Steam heat   Electric bells and lights   THOMAS KILCOUUSE

Hotel Malatesta

Atlantic and North Carolina Avenues

Open all the Year

M. MALATESTA, Proprietor   J. K. CARMACK, Manager

Formerly Girard House, Philadelphia

Hotel Longinotti and Cafe

COR. ILLINOIS AND ATLANTIC AVES.

European Plan

J. R. LONGINOTTI, Proprietor   DAVID LONGINOTTI, Manager

Formerly of Wm. Megonegal's, 1021 Chestnut St., Philadelphia

24

A June Morning on the Boardwalk—Looking Eastward

25

26

The Casino—Looking toward the Boardwalk

27

28

29

30

Irvin's Dry Goods Store—Union National Bank Building

ATLANTIC CITY

Seashore Sketches—Winter and Summer
Attractions—Memoranda and Ready
Reference for Visitors.

By A. M. HESTON.

—

THIRTEENTH YEAR OF PUBLICATION.

Thus recordynge the time passed, I have fulfilled these thynges and putte hem wryten
in this boke, as it would come into my mynde.—SIR JOHN MAUNDEVILLE.

REVISED EDITION.
1899.

Good-bye to pain and care! I take
  Mine ease to-day ;
Here, where the sunny waters break
And ripples this keen breeze, I shake
All burdens from the heart, all weary thoughts away.

Ha ! like a kind hand on my brow
  Comes this fond breeze,
Cooling its dull and feverish glow ;
While through my being seems to flow
The breath of a new life— the healing of the seas.

— *Whittier*

Easter Sunday, 1899, on the Boardwalk

Atlantic City.

There is that lovely island fair,
And the pale health-seeker findeth there
The wine of life in its pleasant air.

TLANTIC CITY, the most popular resort on the Atlantic coast, is situated between Absecon Inlet and Great Egg Harbor Inlet, within sixty miles of Philadelphia and one hundred and fifty miles of New York, by railroad. It is distant five miles from the mainland, the intervening space being an expanse of salt marshes. The island, in its chrysalis condition, before it felt the electric touch of a railroad, was known as Absecon Beach, which name still exists in the adjoining village of Absecon, now put completely in the shade by its successful neighbor, and in the official name of the lighthouse, Absecon Light.

Jeremiah Leeds was probably the first permanent resident of the island. He came here in 1783, when a pair of boots or a roll of calico would have bought the entire island. The early history of Absecon Beach is filled with stories of drowning, piracy and shipwreck. According to tradition, vessels were lured ashore on dark and stormy nights by false beacons erected on poles. When the crews had been drowned

37

Lighthouse and Life Saving Station

or individually knocked on the head, so the stories go, the crafts were plundered of everything of value. One chronicler boldly asserts, with apparent perversion of the truth, that, even after the first church was built, a lookout was added above the cupola, in which a man was stationed during service to promptly acquaint the devout congregation of a disaster, so that rival wreckers in the neighborhood of Barnegat or Brigantine should not get the start of them. Another prevaricating writer says the children were taught to lisp the prayer : "God bless mam, pap, and all us poor, miserable sinners, and send a ship ashore before morning."

Long before the days of railroads Absecon Beach bore the gruesome name among sailors of "Jack's Graveyard." There was no lighthouse then, and often the beach was strewn with wreck, and among the *débris* many a time lay the dead body of a sailor. Over at Absecon they still tell thrilling stories of drowning and shipwreck.

Besides the Leeds family, two other families owned most of the land on which Atlantic City is built—the Steelmans and Chamberlains. The mother of the numerous Leeds progeny kept the old Atlantic House as a tavern for oystermen and traders. It is the oldest house in Atlantic City, and was built about the year 1812, but has since been enlarged. It originally stood near the Thoroughfare at Baltic and Florida Avenues, but was moved to its present site on Baltic Avenue near Massachusetts.

Forty years ago the location of Atlantic City was still an almost uninhabited island. It was so uninviting that when the project to make it a summer resort was instituted, the idea was ridiculed as being utterly impracticable and scarcely worth the consideration of sane men. Said a conservative old capitalist : "Call it a sand-patch, a desolation, a swamp, a mosquito territory, but do not talk to me about any city in such a place as that. In the first place, you can't build a city there, and, in the second place, if you did, you couldn't get anybody to go there." The conservative old capitalist was in due time gathered unto his fathers, and the enterprising men who set to work to plant a city have had the satisfaction of seeing more than their most sanguine expectations realized.

The island began to awaken from its slumbering obscurity in the early part of 1852, when a glass manufacturer of New Jersey, laboring under the difficulties produced by almost impassable roads and consequent delays in the transportation of goods to Philadelphia, conceived the idea of starting a railroad. Besides this plan for increasing his own business facilities, he also proposed to make the new road an outlet from Philadelphia to the sea, as well as a valuable freight transport for a manufac-

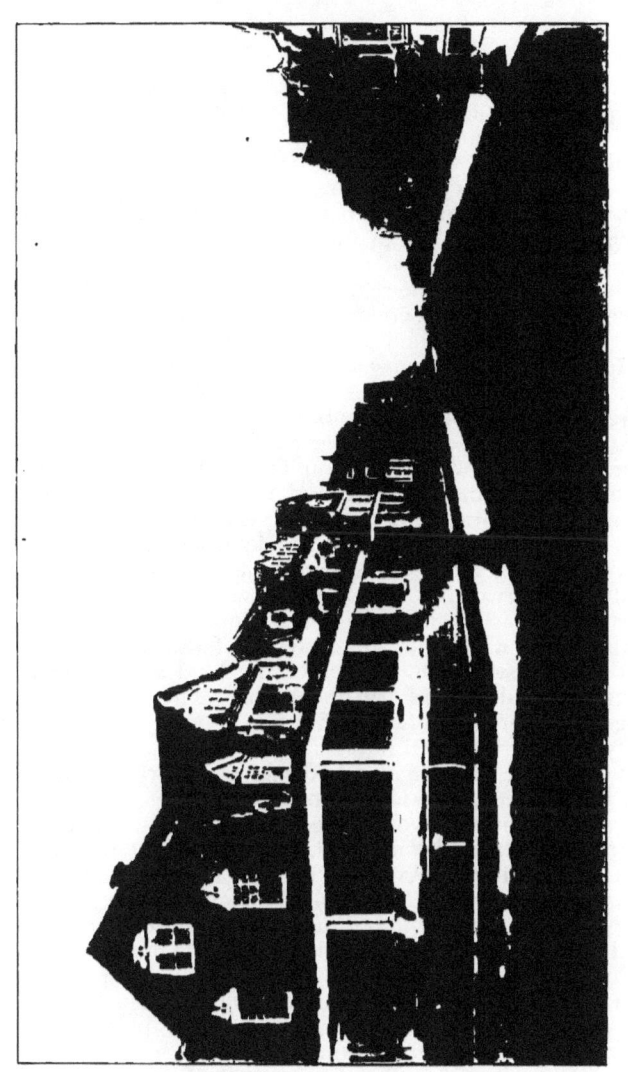

St. Charles Place, looking Seaward

turing district. This was Samuel Richards, the first mover in the creation of Atlantic City. His associates were Hon. Andrew K. Hay, Stephen Colwell, John C. De Costa, Joseph Porter, William Coffin, Enoch Doughty and Dr. Jonathan Pitney, all deceased. The first projecting visit to the solitary marshes and sand-hills of what is now Atlantic City, was made in the early part of 1852 ; an act of incorporation was obtained in the spring, and in September of the same year a contract was made for the construction of the road. The engineer was Richard B. Osborne. The road was completed and passenger trains were run on it for the first time on July 1, 1854. Meanwhile Bedloe's Hotel and a little house called Cottage Retreat had been erected, and the United States Hotel was so nearly completed that the first excursionists, numbering six hundred, were given dinner there. The next year the Surf House, Congress Hall, another hotel, and two cottages on Tennessee Avenue went up. As an adjunct to, and arising out of the railroad company, the Camden and Atlantic Land Company was organized and chartered. This company purchased the land for seventeen dollars and fifty cents per acre. The money was paid over in old Aunt Hannah Shillingworth's Hotel in Absecon. Then began the rise in values that has made so many people rich, though, with the usual irony of fate, the descendants of the original owners and settlers are still poor. Much of the land is now valued at over one hundred dollars per lineal foot. The same land was purchased by Jeremiah Leeds in 1783 at forty cents an acre. The city was incorporated immediately after the purchase of the land, but for the first year or two it took nearly all the men among the permanent residents to fill the offices. Chalkley S. Leeds was the first mayor. The city limits now cover about one-third of the entire island. The original boundary was from the inlet to California Avenue, but the lower limit was afterward extended to " Dry Inlet," or Jackson Avenue.

In 1876 the increasing importance of the place made another railroad desirable, and the Philadelphia and Atlantic City Railroad Company was incorporated. The construction was commenced in April, 1877, and the first through train was run on June 25th of the same year. It is now operated by what is commonly known as the Reading Company, of Philadelphia. The competing facilities offered by this road have been of the greatest benefit to the city, and have aided materially in the development of the place.

Early in the spring of 1880 the West Jersey Division of the Pennsylvania Railroad extended its line to Atlantic City. The opening of the West Jersey was of exceptional benefit to the city, since a direct route to New York city, without change of cars, was thereby afforded.

The nomenclature of the streets of Atlantic City is especially happy. The great main avenues running parallel with the ocean, five hundred and fifty feet apart, have a breezy suggestiveness of coolness in their names—Pacific, Atlantic and Arctic —while the wide thoroughfares that cross them at right angles, bearing the names of the States of the Union, illustrate the patriotism of those who founded the city.

The advancement of Atlantic City since the completion of the three railroads has been unprecedented in the history of watering places and health resorts, even in this progressive country, and suggests a comparison with the magic progress of Chicago or Denver. The city has spread itself literally as well as figuratively, in actual size as well as in population, and the value of property has increased ten-fold. Lots on Atlantic Avenue now sell for from two to three hundred dollars per front foot, and choice lots on Pacific Avenue bring as much as one hundred and twenty-five dollars per foot. The tendency is still upward in every part of the city.

A Relic of the Revolution—Home of General Doughty, on the Mainland.

Whence Came Atlantic City?

I will learn of thee a prayer,
To Him who gave a home so fair,
  A lot so blest as ours—
The God who made for thee and me,
This sweet, fair isle amid the sea.
                —William Cullen Bryant.

IT is apparent that the fame of Atlantic City is grounded not alone upon those qualities which give it prominence as a summer resort. It is a great seaside city, where in every part of the year the health and pleasure seekers crowd the hotels and lounge on its famous beach. In summer the magnificent bathing and the famous fishing and sailing attract thousands; in winter the genial temperature, bright sky and other delightful features make it the stopping place for a grand army of those who seek to escape the rigor of northern climes. There are several good schools, with an attendance of over two thousand school children, Presbyterian, Episcopal, Roman Catholic, Methodist, Baptist and Lutheran churches, and a Friends' Meeting House.

To the inquiry, "Whence came Atlantic City?" we reply: It is a refuge thrown up by the continent building sea. Fashion took a caprice and shook it out of a fold of her flounce. A railroad laid a wager to find the shortest distance from Penn's treaty elm to the Atlantic Ocean; it dashed into the water and a city emerged from its train as a consequence of the manœuvre.

Juan Ponce de Leon, the Spanish explorer of the sixteenth century, sought in vain for the spring whose virtues were credulously believed to restore the vigor of youth to the aged. Searching for this fountain of youth, he landed on the coast of Florida

43

in the year 1512, and in that country there are springs almost innumerable, each of which to-day lays claim to the high antiquity of being the identical spring in which the great Spaniard performed his daily ablutions. History informs us, however, that nowhere could he find this mythical fountain of youth ; but who will deny that had he extended his search northward his fondest hopes might have been realized, had he landed upon this island, where—quoting the lines of Col. William E. Potter, of Bridgeton, N. J.—

Where the long surges heave and break,
Foaming, upon the glittering shore,
And laughing maidens often take
A " header " 'midst the breakers' roar ;
Where zephyrs gently woo the toiler,
And nights are mild an l skies are clear,
And on the housewife's kitchen l roiler
The soft-shell crab doth oft appear ;
Where hops abound and bugles blare,
And Roman nobles, in the busy street,
Incognito, with monkeys fare,
Grinding their daily music sweet ;
Where agile oysters, mild, serene,
On beds of moss recline, and lobsters wise
Live pinchingly ; and pearly sheen
Of hake and flounder wins the flies ;
And the mosquito's monotone,
Beyond the woven window-bar,
Prevents our feeling quite alone—
He is so near and yet so far ;
Where, by the heaving sea, the fakir's booth
Is found ere yet the summer's gone,
Pours forth the fountain of eternal youth,
The spring of ancient Ponce Leon.

The old Castilian left his home,
The vine-clad hills of distant Spain,
A thousand leagues of sea to roam ;
To brave the heat, the cold, the pain
Of wounds, the fatal poisoned dart,
The march through swamp and tangled wood,
The ambush dark, the fear, the start
Of keen surprise when the wild Indian stood,
Stern, painted, cruel, before him,
But undismayed by wounds or death,
His loved lost youth to restore him,
Aged, weak and worn, with failing breath,
He searched, without the glorious sight
Of the famed spring, now flowing free,
Pure and wholesome, sparkling and bright,
In our gay City by the Sea.

The old Castilian died long before the feet of white men trod the soil whereon Atlantic City was founded, but the wonderful

The Boardwalk—Westward from the Casino

life-giving atmosphere of this beach, if not the identical "spring of youth," was discovered by a writer on climatology, in the eighteenth century, who speaks of the "exceptional dryness of the atmosphere on Absecon beach," and adds that "there is only one other spot on the seacoast, anywhere in the world, which is comparable to this in that respect."

Atlantic City truly is a place of rest, and for those in quest of health, an equable climate in winter, and refreshing breezes in summer ; for those who would enjoy the invigorating sea air and be charmed with the music of the surf ; for those who would delight in the pleasures of yachting or fishing ; for those who would have long life, good living, good society, and be inspired by the grandeur of old ocean ; for those who, like Ponce de Leon, would discover the place which imparts youth to the aged, health to the sick, and hope to the despondent, there is no more highly favored spot anywhere in the land than this beautiful City by the Sea.

Some of the advantages of Atlantic City over other resorts may be thus stated :

Its hotels are among the finest and most comfortable on the coast.

It has a perfect system of sanitation.

It has an abundant water supply from artesian wells and from natural springs on the mainland.

Its death rate is smaller than that of most other cities of the country.

It has a property valuation of nearly fifteen millions.

It is lighted with gas and electricity, and has a first-class volunteer fire department, with several engines and hose carriages, and two hook and-ladder trucks.

It has ample telegraph and telephone facilities.

It has excellent schools and churches, good society, good people and good living.

It has an efficient police force for the preservation of peace. Discipline is well maintained, and even in the most crowded weeks of summer there is no disorder.

Several physicians, of eminence in their profession, are resident here.

Ivigorating hot and cold sea-water baths are furnished at many of the hotels, and at establishments specially erected for that purpose.

Electric lights at night render the streets as bright as day Electric cars run the length of the main business thoroughfare, and carriage hire is so cheap as to astonish visitors accustomed to the extortions of the Jehus who infest some other resorts.

Cottage of George Kelley   Residence of Hon. Lewis Evans   Residence of Dr. G. W. Crosby

Pennsylvania Avenue School—Texas Avenue School—Indiana
Avenue School

Old Ocean's Invitation.

How sweet the memory of the sea,
Pictured in beauty, comes to me,
  The peopled strand, the waves that rise
To where the sunbeams sweetly play—
  The storm-cloud gathering in the skies,
Crowned with wild glory, and away,
Rocked on the bosom of the sea,
A light craft speeding joyously.

To me its music sweetness seems,
Like music of entrancing dreams,
  Its power, mysterious and grand,
Steals o'er my spirit as a spell;
  I wander on the drifted sand,
And hear the songs the billows tell;
I read a well-taught lesson there
Of life and light divinely fair,

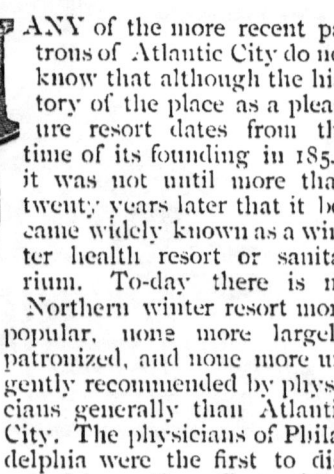

MANY of the more recent patrons of Atlantic City do not know that although the history of the place as a pleasure resort dates from the time of its founding in 1854, it was not until more than twenty years later that it became widely known as a winter health resort or sanitarium. To-day there is no Northern winter resort more popular, none more largely patronized, and none more urgently recommended by physicians generally than Atlantic City. The physicians of Philadelphia were the first to discover the wonderful curative effects of the saline air of Atlantic City, and to them, more than to any other class of men, is due the credit of making the city what it is—a famous sanitarium. Overtaxed brains are ordered hither by

49

Dr. S. Weir Mitchell, the man who has the honor of having discovered the "rest cure." He and his learned congeners have found that many chronic diseases result from nervous exhaustion. The sufferer from incipient paralysis or brain·

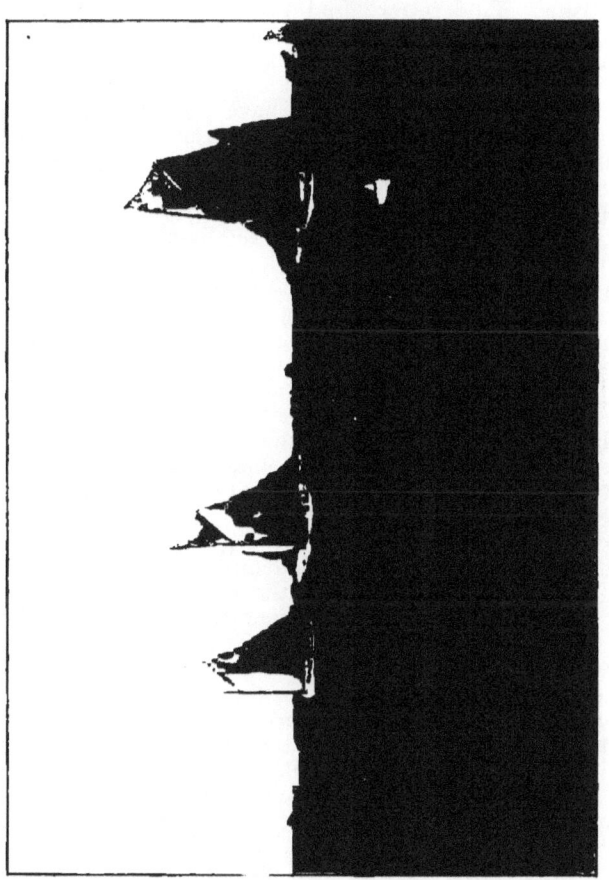

Yachting Scene at the Inlet

softening is ordered to Atlantic City for six months, and in many instances returns to his home cured. It was N. P. Willis who first said that "consumption is curable if the patient can stop consuming." The once dreaded disease to which every New England woman resigned herself fifty years ago, if her lungs began to trouble her, is as curable now as the measles, if taken in time.

In old times the seashore was considered a desolate place in winter. Such a bleak idea as to be there in the snow months, and amid storms of ice and sleet, would have chilled the marrow of an invalid. And yet we find this place a very sanitarium for the sick during the winter. Victims of sore throats and of lung diseases have found the bracing air of Atlantic City better than all the doctor-stuff they could swallow at home. Many of the wealthy, who otherwise would have gone to Europe, have spared themselves the annoyances of ocean travel by settling down here for a few months. Many who used to go to Florida in winter now find Atlantic City all they desire.

Of the many thousands who visit Atlantic City in the interval between the first of January and the first of June, it is not to be supposed that all are in search of health. As has been already hinted, a three-fold object is associated with life at this resort at that season. Invalids, especially those troubled with bronchial affections or convalescing from malarial attacks, following the advice of their physicians, come here to regain their wonted health and strength ; others whose daily life of care and toil has brought on nervous exhaustion seek rest and recuperation where it is generally to be found ; and others still, following the bent of fashion, are to be found among the throng of pleasure seekers who hie themselves hither during the Lenten season.

In winter, when the majority of the guests are invalids, any but the mildest forms of dissipation are, of course, out of the question ; but during Lent, when the more extravagant gayeties of the rest of the world are temporarily suspended, Atlantic City becomes the scene of genuine fun and frolic.

Lenten parties for Atlantic City are formed in the larger cities. Upon the advent of Lent some good-natured married lady, of unimpeachable social standing, organizes a party of from a dozen to twenty young people, and offers to chaperon them to Atlantic City. They go for a week or ten days, often staying longer, and while they are here the heretofore quiet hotels ring with the sounds of music, dancing and merry laughter. The more sober-minded invalids gaze with a mild surprise, not unmixed with pleasure, at these jolly parties, and by force of example become more energetic and inclined to forget their ailments.

In considering Atlantic City as a winter and spring resort, it is proper to offer some explanation of the causes which produce such beneficial results. To this end we must have recourse to the opinions of leading physicians and scientists who have made a careful study of the matter. "Actual experience," says Dr.

Boardman Reed in the *Medical Times*, "has demonstrated that sea air is as valuable in winter as in summer. It also bears out the statistics which prove that the climate of Atlantic City is superior to that of most seacoast towns, being drier, more equable and unusually mild, considering the latitude." The same authority says: "Another peculiarity of the location of Atlantic City is that all the winds from the landward must pass for long distances—hundreds of miles in some directions—over a very dry and porous sandy soil, upon which snow rarely lies for any time. These winds, including those from the north, northwest, west and southwest are, therefore, to some extent, both dried and warmed in their passage. Though the coast of Southern New Jersey has a general direction from northeast to southwest, the beach at Atlantic City trends more to the westward, so that it faces almost directly southward. Therefore south as well as east winds are sea breezes here, and both blow across the Gulf Stream, which exercises considerable influence upon the climate of this part of the coast."

A well-known physician of Baltimore, the late Dr. J. T. King, says: "The geological peculiarity of the island is one of the agents that contribute to the remarkable healthfulness of Atlantic City at all seasons of the year. There is no indigenous or spontaneous vegetation upon the island. The only growth to be seen is the arboreal embellishments of the avenues and lawns—sylvan contributions from the forests of the mainland. No stagnant pools or sloughs mar or disfigure the facial lineaments of the island, and there is no malarial or miasmatic emanation or effluvium to offend the senses or to affect its perfect hygiene."

'Tis the pearly shell,
That murmurs of the far off murmuring sea;
A precious jewel, carved most curiously—
It is a little picture painted well.

—R. W. GILDER.

Oldest Hotel in Atlantic City, near Turnpike Bridge

"The Healing of the Seas."

Good-bye to pain and care! I take
  Mine ease to-day;
Here, where the sunny waters break
And ripples this keen breeze, I shake
All burdens from the heart, all weary thoughts away.

Ha! like a kind hand on my brow
  Comes this fond breeze,
Cooling its dull and feverish glow;
While through my being seems to flow
The breath of a new life—the healing of the seas.
                        WHITTIER.

DOUBTLESS several elements combine to produce the resting and tonic effect of the sea air, the first of which is the presence of a large amount of ozone—the stimulating, vitalizing principle of the atmosphere. Ozone has a tonic, healing and purifying power that increases as the air is taken into the lungs. It strengthens the respiratory organs, and in stimulating them helps the whole system. It follows naturally that the blood is cleansed and revivified, tone is given to the stomach, the liver is excited to healthful action, and the whole body feels the benefit. Perfect health is the inevitable result, if there be enough of the constitution left to build upon.

The saline particles held in suspension in the atmosphere, the "dust of the ocean," enter the system through the lungs, and aid in the tonic effect experienced at the seashore. But whatever may be the cause, the effect is undoubted. Few who visit Atlantic City fail to experience a marked improvement in appetite, while to many there comes such a feeling icines—trustworthy evidence as to what they have accomplished is the most valuable. With regard to nervous, rheumatic, gouty, dyspeptic and various other chronic ailments which are usually found to be benefited here in the summer, equal benefit may be expected in the winter. Convalescents from acute diseases or from surgical operations nearly always improve remarkably upon being removed to Atlantic City from the large cities.

"As to diseases of the respiratory organs," says Dr. Reed, "I have had personal knowledge of many patients suffering from various forms of such affections who have made trials of this climate in winter. The cases have, as a rule, improved, some of them very decidedly, though there have been exception. The consumptives who were in the incipient stage, and those even in the advanced stages where the destructive process has been advancing slowly, have often experienced very marked improvement. In a considerable proportion—about one fourth —of the cases of the latter class, the disease has been apparently arrested, and some of them seem to be cured."

It is a significant fact that pneumonia and bronchitis are of infrequent origin here, and when they do occur the patients almost invariably recover. Upon this point Dr. Reed's experience as a resident physician enables him to speak very positively. He has not known an uncomplicated attack of either disease to prove fatal.

To another highly respected physician, Dr. James Darrach, of Germantown, belongs the honor of having relieved many patients suffering from hay fever and autumnal catarrh by sending them to Atlantic City. The late Rev. H. W. Beecher and Dr. Oliver Wendell Holmes had a witty correspondence on the subject of hay fever, in which the latter declared that there was no cure for the disease "but six feet of gravel." Atlantic City, however, has answered back that, if it cannot be cured, it may at least be alleviated.

Nature has provided Atlantic City with the health-giving sea; with a balmy and delightful climate; with a sandy soil, which, after a light snow or heavy rain, dries with marvelous quickness. Come, then, ye who seek health, rest or pleasure; come and fill your lungs with the ozone of the sea; come and promenade on the four-mile boardwalk planted within reach of the spray; come and sit in a rocking-chair and take a sun-bask in the open air or in one of the several Ocean Parlors; come before it gets too warm; come while ye may; come *now*. Take no heed of a chronic fault-finder who may be here, enjoying to the full all the benefits and advantages of Atlantic City and the hospitalities of its people, and who still carps and grumbles because the town lacks a few pretty curves and graces.

Hotel Brighton—South View

Summmer Days by the Sea.

O Summer day beside the joyous sea!
O Summer day so wonderful and white,
So full of gladness and so full of pain!
Forever and forever shalt thou be
To some the gravestone of a dead delight,
To some the landmark of a new domain.
—LONGFELLOW.

RAND and glorious are the summer days beside the sea! Scarcely has passed the brief period of transition from the austere days of December to the balmy weather of May, ere one's thoughts revert, with fond remembrance, to the delightful scenes, the cool and invigorating breezes, and the joyous pastimes of Atlantic City, where the summer's day of the poet is something more than a mere creation of the fancy.

The oft-quoted lines of George Herbert, the sweet singer of Cherbury—

" Sweet day, so cool, so calm, so bright,
The bridal of the earth and sky,"—

are almost meaningless to those who know summer only from the high temperatures, the glaring sun and the hot, parching winds that are its distinguishing characteristics in no inconsiderable portion of the United States.

The ideal summer presupposes climatic conditions that make physical life—from the highest to the lowest—a perpetual delight and rejoicing ; and, if there is any place more favored than another in that regard, it must surely be a matter of concern to the toiling millions to know where it may be found.

But, apart from the mere pursuit of pleasure, the mere seeking after enjoyment, and that love of change for its own sake

57

that is inherent in every son of Adam, there is, happily, in this busy, restless age, a just recognition of the importance of relaxing the extreme tension of business and endeavoring to repair the terrible waste of vital force. We are, however, with our pleasures very much what we are in our business, except that while we may not always make a pleasure of our business, we certainly make a business of our pleasure, seeking to obtain, with the least outlay, the largest possible results.

The accessibility of a summer resort is, therefore, with not a few, a matter of importance, second only to the paramount consideration of health and pleasure ; and herein lies the secret of Atlantic City's wonderful growth and popularity.

The first-class hotels and numerous boarding-houses in Atlantic City are overtaxed in summer-time to accommodate those who come from every direction, north, east, south and west. Cottages have sprung up with a rapidity and in numbers without a parallel in the history of any other resort in the world. These cottages find occupants in the spring, most of whom remain until October.

The solid character of its patrons from the better elements of society, the quiet, home-like aspect of the place, the natural scenery and charms peculiar to itself conspire to make Atlantic City the very ideal of a summer resort. Art and design have added to its attractions, beautifying it with broad avenues, with walks bordered with trees, and with gardens whose fragrance unites with the cool breeze of the ocean to delight and refresh those who seek rest and recreation at the seashore.

The summer brings its own amusements, and Atlantic City has been so blessed by Providence that nature provides a constant round of pleasures. The sea is a source of endless delight. The bathing in the pure surf, free from every defilement, is superb, and its invigorating pleasures are enjoyed by nearly all except the weakest of the invalid visitors. Even those who do not bathe find a pleasure in sitting under big umbrellas on the beach, and watching the antics of those who are tumbling in the surf.

For sailing under the most favorable conditions, the Inlet affords ample opportunity, and good boats, ably manned by veteran seamen, are always to be had at a fair price. The Inlet is the favorite resort of the lovers of those twin sports, yachting and fishing. A large fleet of handsome yachts is always riding at anchor in waiting for parties desirous for a sail over the briny waters, or of indulging in that exciting sport, deep-sea fishing. The water is, at times, fairly alive with game fish, such as sea bass, flounders, weak fish, king fish, porgies, croakers, snapping mackerel, blue fish and kindred varieties. The most delicious oysters are to be had here, fresh from their native beds, and

Residence of A. M. Jordan—Snellenberg Cottage, States Avenue—Academy of
the Sacred Heart

with an appetizing flavor unknown to one who has never eaten
them before the moss of their shells is dry. The Thoroughfare,
which is as smooth as a mountain lake, is another favorite resort, especially for the ladies. It abounds in crabs, which are
caught in great numbers. Those who prefer steam to sails as a
motor can be accommodated also, and the few whose stomachs
dread the heaving billows may eschew both and idly sit and
watch the fleet of gayly decked boats as they dance in the dim
distance with their precious freight, their blood meanwhile
tingling with the ozone blown from the sea, or the commoner
kind which some endeavor to suck through a straw.

After the pleasures of the day are done there is abundant
dancing. Many of the hotels retain orchestras for the season,
and hops go on every evening. Concerts and plays offer their
own attractions, and there is an infinite variety of other diversions. Indeed, it is impossible to pass a dull day or evening,
and yet, if you care nothing for the sprightlier pleasures, you
may be as quiet as you please, and find delight in meeting and
chatting with friends and communing with the sea.

In addition to the customary weekly hops at the principal
hotels, Atlantic City is visited during the summer season by
some of the best musical and dramatic talent, and concerts and
entertainments are given at the Grand Opera House. These,
in connection with the varied and ever-recurring pleasures natural to the resort, present a constant round of enjoyment.

Life, indeed, at Atlantic City during the summer is, in one
aspect, without restraint. Coming from every part of the land
and from every walk in life, the crowd must necessarily be a
motley one, but there is none of that "respect of persons"
which is sometimes seen in the churches. The man with a "gold
ring, in goodly apparel," is not considered one whit better than
the "poor man in vile raiment;" indeed, appearances are so
deceptive that it would never be safe to judge of the size of a
man's bank account by the clothes he has on—especially if it
be a bathing suit. Men whose talents have made them famous
throughout the land—judges, lawyers and ministers—arrayed
in a suit of blue and white, mingle daily with the other bathers,
ignorant of who they are and regardless of their social standing. It is no uncommon sight to see men eminent in their call-
ings busily engaged in scooping up bucketfuls of sand for children whom they chance to meet upon the beach, or aiding them
in their search for shells after a receding tide. Sedate bachelors
and prudish old maids not infrequently take part in such diversions as these, and, viewing the scenes from the calm of a pavilion, one cannot help thinking that the intellects and the
characters thus unbent, and finding a share in the enjoyments
of childhood, appear to greater advantage by the relaxation.

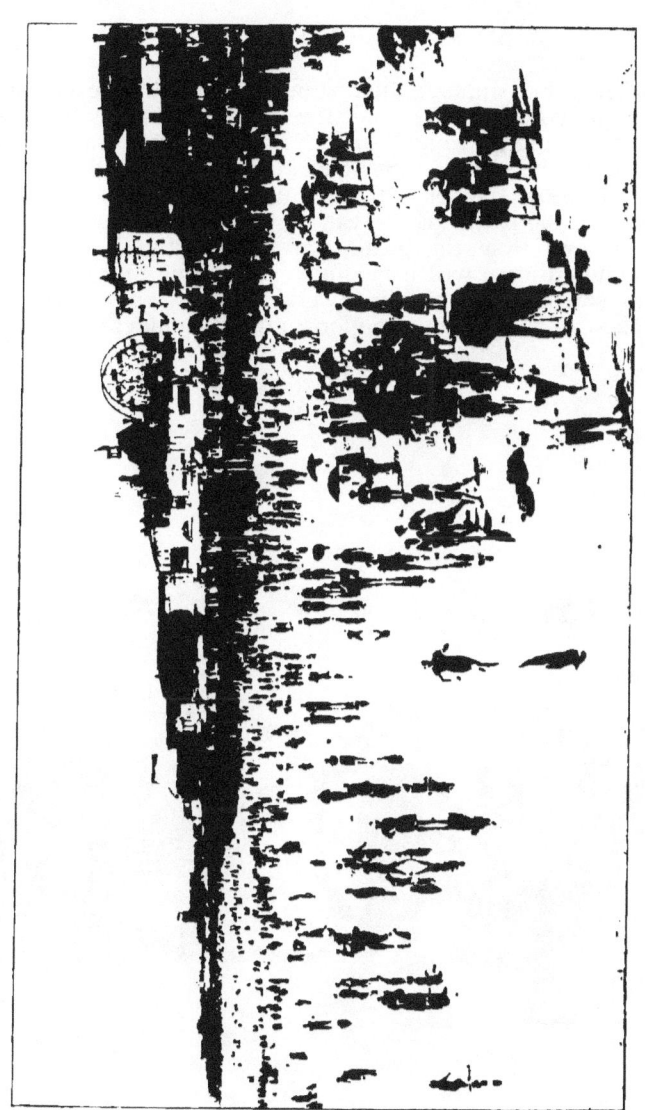

The Strand on a June Morning

Year after year, summer after summer, this strange commingling of the young and the old, the high and the low, the rich and the poor, the grave and the gay, goes on in Atlantic City; and so until the end of time, generation after generation, the charmed voice of the sea will draw men to its sands and to its surf. From the plains of the South, from the wide expanse of the West, and from the bleak, gray rim of the North, men, women and children will come and go, girdling our coast with joy and sorrow through the twelve months—months which make possible the winter's comfort and the summer's pleasure.

Boardwalk and Strand.

Love the sea?   I dote upon it—from the beach.
—DOUGLAS JERROLD.

TLANTIC CITY invented the boardwalk, and while other resorts have been content to tamely copy it, Atlantic City has lengthened and strengthened, rebuilt and renewed, until the present "Boardwalk," erected in the spring and early summer of 1896, is forty feet wide, twelve feet high, and four miles long. It is constructed of steel, cost the city nearly $150,000, and is the only structure of the kind in the world.

When one is tired or wants to study humanity, there is no place equal to the Boardwalk. As a study of some of the most unique phases of human character, a stroll along this crowded thoroughfare is worth a year of ordinary life. Its infinite variety preserves it from monotony, and never does it present the same aspect two days in succession.

The life, the light and the color that one sees on this promenade during the early hours of a summer evening are indescribable. It is an endless dress parade, a grand review in which everybody is one of the reviewers as well as one of the reviewed. The animation, the overflowing good-nature, the laughter and contagious hilarity of this restless throng are irresistible. The lights from the scores of bazaars, the buoyant merriment of countless children, the soft, melting colors of the summer dresses of the women, the grace and freshened loveliness of the

62

A Summer Afternoon at the Inlet Wharf

women themselves, the dizzy whirl of the merry-go-round, the toboggan, the switchback, the figure-eight or the round-about and the thousand and one little scraps of life and tone that line the thoroughfare blend in a picture which is warranted to banquet the eye and rest the mind of any man who has not utterly lost the capacity for being entertained, and all to the soothing accompaniment of the caressing airs and the thunderous monotone of the blue, unresting sea.

At the lower end of the city, at a point known as Seaview, there is a spacious new hotel, specially designed for excursionists—that is, persons who come down to spend a day at the sea-shore. This class aggregates many thousands. The house is

Watching the "Sandman"

provided with a well-appointed restaurant, pleasant parlors, broad piazzas, a merry-go-round and a spacious ball-room. Starting from the vicinity of the Seaview Excursion House and following the Boardwalk in the direction of the Inlet, the pedestrian comes to the lighthouse, situated at the northeastern end of the island, near the entrance to Absecon Inlet.

From the balcony of the lighthouse a grand panorama of sea and land is presented. We behold there what the world looks like to a sea-gull ; and a grand waste of waters it seems, indeed. Looking north and west, across the extended miles of salt meadows, with their winding thoroughfares and bays, one sees the lines of pretty buildings and the fertile farms of the mainland.

Stretching to the southwest is the beautiful city, with its grand hotels, its extensive boarding-houses, its hundreds of private cottages embowered in shrubbery and the long line of shade-trees skirting the sidewalks; while beyond, to the east and south, the ocean stretches into the distant horizon.

There is nothing which inspires the mind of man like the lighthouses, which, crowning the headlands along shore, flash their warnings one to another and far out to sea, telling the sailor not only of his approach to land but of his position at sea also. John Quincy Adams said he never saw these coast-lights in the evening without recalling to mind the light that Columbus saw flashing from shore the night he discovered the New World.

Many delightful, dreamy hours may be spent upon the strand during the day when the weather is pleasant. The long stretch of sandy beach and the roar of the surf may be uninteresting to some upon a gloomy day, but when the sun is shining all dreariness disappears, the ocean sparkles like a huge diamond, and groups of people wander along the strand or scoop out convenient hollows, in which they lie for hours, enjoying the warm sun-bath and inhaling ozone at every breath. Bevies of girls dressed in dainty costumes are scattered about on the sand, and ripples of laughter come to one's ears from every side. Far out upon the horizon a faint trace of smoke may be seen ascending from a passing steamer, while above the horizon and sometimes just beyond the surf the white wings of swift-sailing yachts or other craft lend a charm and a motion to the scene. Nothing could add to the quiet beauty of this scene or heighten the pleasure of those for whom it is created.

From morning until evening the beach is a perfect paradise for children. The youngsters take to digging in the sand and paddling in the water by natural instinct, having unlimited opportunities for both. Every day they throw up fortifications, build mounds and excavate subterranean caverns, and every night the tide washes away all their labor and leaves a soft, smooth surface for another day's toil.

The pleasures of the surf bath bring multitudes to Atlantic City during the summer months, and bathing here attains a popularity unknown to more northern resorts, the near approach of the Gulf Stream to this point increasing the temperature of the water to a delightful degree, and taking from it the bitter chill from which so many would-be bathers shrink. At the fashionable hours of bathing, from eleven to one, the beach is crowded with thousands of merry bathers, whose shouts and laughter mingle with the roar of the surf, while the strand and Boardwalk are lined with interested spectators and promenaders. The scene at this time is as animated as the streets of a conti-

Old Catawba Church, near May's Landing—Central M. E. Church

nental city on a *fête* day. At night when the electric lights
are lit and the Boardwalk is thronged with merry promenaders,
Atlantic City presents a picture of delightful existence, fairer
than any vision of a midsummer night's dream.

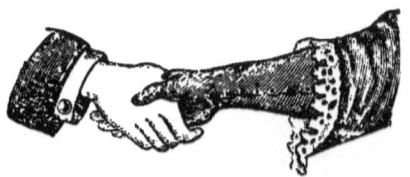

THE AUTUMN BREAK-UP—THEY MAY
NEVER MEET AGAIN,

Iron Pier, Hauling in the Seine and Bathing Scene

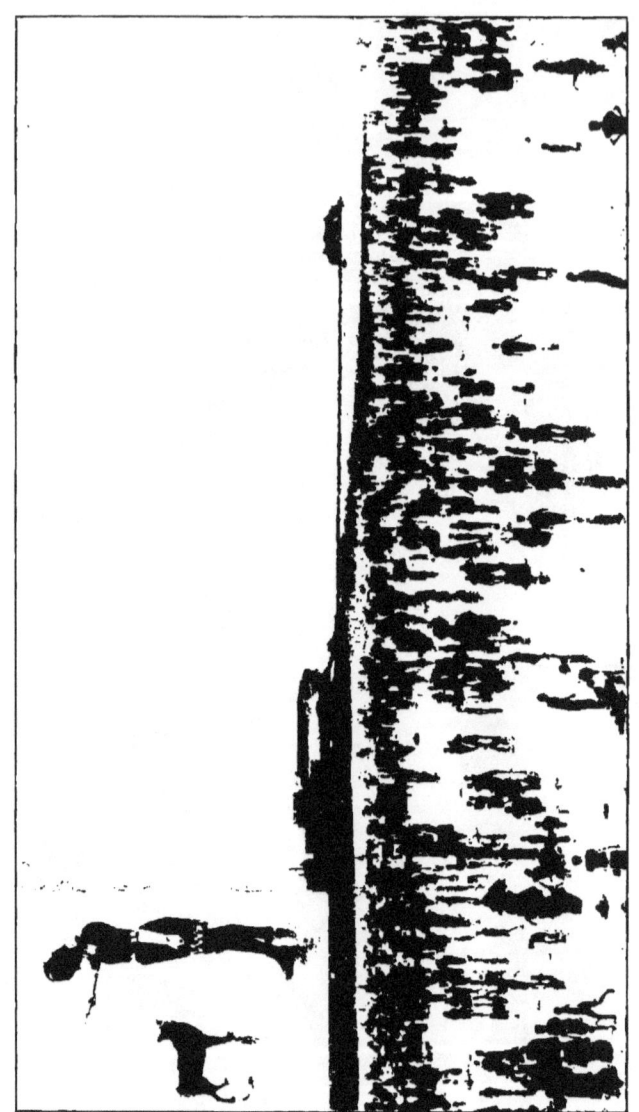

Bathing Scene in July

Gunning and Fishing.

We may say of fishing, as Dr. Boteler said of strawberries: "Doubtless God could have made a better berry, but He never did," and so, if I may be the judge, God never did make a more calm, quiet and innocent recreation than fishing.— ISAAK WALTON.

NOWHERE else along the coast are there greater facilities for sport with the rod and the gun than in the vicinity of Atlantic City. The bays and thoroughfares are a vast water preserve, with Nature for their keeper. From Grassy Bay and Little Egg Harbor on the north to Great Egg Harbor and Lake's Bay on the south, from the wreck of the "Cassandra" to the wreck of the "Diverty," fish of large size and fowl of many kind are found in abundance. The thoroughfares, sounds and bays teem with millions of the finny tribe at certain seasons of the year, while the woods on the mainland, or "off-shore," if we may use the local vernacular, are splendid feeding grounds for quail in the fall months. The meadows also abound with duck, geese, plover, snipe, marlin, curlew and marsh-hens. Nowhere can the hunter or angler go amiss. It is generally safe to carry the gun or the line, for the fruits thereof will amply repay the drudgery. The waters of the sea and bays and the outlying marshes and woodland contain enough to keep the fisherman and hunter in keen quest after their game

A favorite feeding ground for the robin-breast, or robin-snipe, is the sod beach on Brigantine. An old hunter says that for fifteen years he shot them on this spot from behind a blind near Smith's hotel before daybreak, catching a bead on their

nimble bodies only when the white comb of a breaker flashed in
the background.

Curlews, both of the long bill and crooked bill varieties, are
in good flight in the spring and fall of the year. The latter are
called on the shore horse foot curlews, from a habit they have of
eating the eggs of the king or horse-shoe crab.

Every variety of beach bird can be bagged in the spring, if
the sportsman is speedily on the ground, and a few straggling
birds may be killed as late as the 15th of June. The gunning

Home of the "Atlantis Club," Illinois Avenue.

is equally good in the fall, when the birds make their annual
flight southward. September is generally a good month to test
the sportsman's mettle and skill, and, with perseverance, he is
sure to return laden with small game. Nor will he need any
soothing syrup to woo his natural rest ; his peregrinations will
bring him both appetite, fatigue and stamina. Woodcock may
be killed in July, October and November, plover after August
1st, and marsh-hens after August 25th. For extra sport in
wing shot in the spring and fall the sportsman must visit Grassy
Bay, which is convenient of access by yachts from the Inlet,

where wild duck, brant and geese are found in superior numbers. At low water this bay falls dry, and for an area of many square miles is a feeding ground for every kind of fowl that is common to salt water. Here is found the blue-bill, the black duck, the long-neck, the red-head, the dipper, the cub head, the widgeon, the granny and the shelldrake. Marlin, willet, plover, robin-snipe, graybacks, calico-backs, black breast and all other snipe are also to be found upon the bars of this bay.

Besides Grassy Bay, there is good gunning in Atlantic County in and around Little Bay, Reed's Bay, Absecon Bay, Eagle Bay, Duck Thoroughfare, Newfound Water, Dole's Island, Mankiller Bay, Gull Island Cove, Oyster Thoroughfare Islands, Shelter Islands, Jonas' Island, Pook Island and Lake's Bay.

There is usually very good quail and rabbit shooting in the woods and fields on the mainland.   This is

In the brilliant autumn-time, the most brilliant of all,
When the gorgeous woods are gleaming, ere the leaves begin to fall;
When the maple boughs are crimson, and the hickory shines like gold,
When the noons are sultry hot, and the nights are frosty cold.

When the country has no green, but the sword-grass on the rill,
And the willows in the valley, and the pine upon the hill;
When the pippin leaves the bough, and the sumac's fruit is red,
And the quail is piping loud, from the buckwheat where he fed.

When the sky is blue as steel, and the river clear as glass,
When the mist is on the ocean, and the network on the grass;
When the harvests are all housed, and the farmer's work is done,
And the woodland is resounding with the spaniel and the gun.

The following information will be of permanent value to those who may wish to go in quest of any of the varieties of fish or fowl which are found here at certain seasons of the year:

FISH.

BLUE-FISH.—Appear about the middle of May; leave in October.

SHEEPSHEAD.—Appear about the 10th of June; leave in October,

WEAK-FISH.—Appear in May; leave in October.

STRIPED BASS.—Found in the rivers on the coast the entire winter; more plentiful in summer.

WHITE PERCH.—Come early and remain late; chiefly found in brackish waters and in rivers.

BLACK FISH.—Bite from 1st of June, and cease 1st of October.

New Jersey Avenue School—Chelsea School

SEA BASS.—Taken first of June until October.

KING FISH.—Come in July and remain until October.

FLOUNDERS (SUMMER).—Oblong in shape ; come in June ; stay until October.

FLOUNDERS (WINTER).—Flounder proper ; come in October ; leave in May.

PORGIES.— Abundant along the coast after July.

SPOT, OR GOODY.—Summer fish.

CODFISH.—Taken late in autumn and in winter.

FOWL.

WILD GEESE AND BRANT.—Arrive about the 1st of October and remain until the last of March.

BLACK DUCKS.—Arrive late in September and remain until the 1st of April. They are sometimes seen here in summer.

BROAD BILLS.—Arrive about the 15th of October.

CUB HEADS, DIPPERS AND RED HEADS.—Habits similar to broad bills. Arrive in October and remain until April 1st.

GRAY DUCKS AND TEAL.—Arrive September 1st, leave in November ; come again for a short time in spring on their northern migration.

ENGLISH SNIPE.—Make their appearance about the 1st of April, remain but a short time, go north, and return in October on their way south.

WILSON SNIPE, ROBIN SNIPE, CURLEWS AND YELLOW LEGS.—Come about the 1st of May, make short stay, return in July, and remain till October.

WILLETT.—Willetts remain and breed in salt marshes.

PLOVER.—The several varieties arrive in May, remaining during the summer.

TELL-TALES.—Arrive in May and pass northward ; return in autumn for a short stay.

But remember that there are in New Jersey certain enactments which must be respected. They are known as " Game Laws." They prohibit persons who are gunning for geese, brant or ducks from placing their decoys further off from the edge of the marsh, island, bar, bank, blind or ice than three rods' distance. All persons are prohibited from pursuing any fowl after night with a light. This class of sportsmen are called " pot hunters," and are held in disrepute by legitimate sportsmen.

The fish most taken hereabouts are the weak-fish, king-fish, flounder, sheepshead, sea bass, black-fish and the Cape May goodies. The weak-fish are the most sought after, and are caught nearly everywhere ; being gamy, they afford sport to the professional angler as well as the novice. The bass are more easily caught, and, having a large mouth, they frequently swallow the bait, hook and all, and are caught with less skill than any other fish. The king-fish, when hooked, is a gamy fellow, but is apt to take off the bait and leave the angler's hook bare. The sheepshead usually bites well, but is slow in taking the bait in his mouth, and even after being hooked, one is not sure of him. In the

TROLLING FOR BLUE-FISH.

first place, he is very strong, and if you attempt to pull him in by main strength and awkwardness, the chances are that he will break your line. The custom among experienced fishermen is to drown him out—that is, let him have his own way until exhausted, and then haul him in. The flounder is a nice fish to catch, and bites voraciously. For outside fishing, a trip to either of the sunken wrecks will give the angler fine sport in bass, weak-fish, and sheepshead fishing.

These twin sports of fin and feather are not only delightful in themselves, but they serve the better purpose of aiding largely in restoring health and strength. The conditions are perfect for this way of roughing it; and the invalid, if strong enough to bear the slight fatigue, will speedily find relief, if not a cure, for the ailments to which his flesh is heir. Good digestion, active nutrition and sound sleep restore the nervous system, and these are largely obtained by a moderate indulgence in those exhilarating sports, gunning and fishing. Days and weeks may be spent in cruising about through the bays and thoroughfares, with never a flagging or failing of interest, or lack of occupation which is at the same time enjoyment. And while the bronze deepens on the cheek, and the pulse bounds more vigorously, and the step grows more elastic, there is no thought of yearning for other scenes, but rather of frequent regret that the vacation must soon end.

Boardwalk above Pennsylvania Avenue

Around and About.

T O Atlantic City belongs the credit of having introduced what is now a feature of a dozen seaside resorts—the Boardwalk. This was first built in 1870, five thousand dollars being raised for that purpose. The venture was regarded in an unfavorable light by many of the conservative citizens, some of whom were large owners of real estate, but the younger men carried the project through.

There was no way at that time for the city to pay for this proposed improvement, but city scrip was issued and held by Brown & Woelpper, owners of the United States Hotel, and lumber merchants in Philadelphia. The agreement was that they were to use the scrip for the payment of their taxes and license. Subsequently $5000 of city bonds were sold at a discount of 10 per cent., and with this money the Boardwalk was paid for. The bonds were redeemed by the city about three years later. This walk was eight feet wide, and was completed on June 26, 1870.

The second walk was built by authority of a resolution passed by City Council in September, 1879. On October 2d the contract for its erection was awarded to Henry Disston & Sons, of Philadelphia, and it was completed the following spring. It was sixteen feet wide. This walk was destroyed by severe storms in the winter of 1883-4, but was rebuilt in a more substantial manner in the spring of 1884, at a cost of less than ten thousand dollars. Five years later (September 10, 1889), another storm made almost a complete wreck of the walk, but before another summer it was rebuilt wider, higher and stronger than ever, with an unobstructed view on the seaward side. The completion of this fourth walk was celebrated with a grand torchlight and fireworks procession of citizens, secret societies, militia and firemen, on the night of May 10, 1890, just eight months, to the day, after its destruction. The total cost of this improvement, including the purchase of land and buildings by condemnation, lawyers' fees, &c., was $53,928.50.

In February, 1896, the act of 1889, by authority of which the last Boardwalk had been erected, was amended. It authorized a much greater expenditure and provided for a structure of steel, iron or wood. The walk then in use being too narrow and practically worn out, Council decided to erect a new one of steel. The contract was awarded to the Phœnix Bridge Company, of Philadelphia, and work was begun on April 24, 1896. The formality of a public dedication of this new walk was observed on July 8, 1896, when the golden nail was driven by Mrs. Stoy, wife of the Mayor. There was a "grand rally" on the lawn or park opposite the Hotel Brighton, with speeches by Congressman Gardner and others. In the evening there was a parade of citizens, military companies and fire companies, on the Boardwalk, and fireworks galore. The walk was not entirely completed until the following September, having a temporary railing during most of the summer. The entire cost, including legal expenses, was $143,986.38. The Chelsea extension of this walk was built in the spring of 1898, at a cost of $14,070.76, and the Inlet extension was partially rebuilt in the spring of 1899 at a cost of $8000.

By a resolution passed August 17, 1896, the name of "Boardwalk" was officially given to the present elevated structure on the beach front of Atlantic City. There is no authority for the word "esplanade," sometimes used by uninformed persons in referring to this promenade. The word is a misnomer.

This walk, now about four miles in length, and extending from the Inlet to Seaview, is the distinctive feature of Atlantic City. It follows the contour of the beach just above the line of high water, and is lighted with the electric lights its entire length. In summer time, when the beach is crowded and the promenade thronged with pedestrians, Atlantic City presents a scene of gayety unequaled anywhere else in the country.

Atlantic City Hospital.—About the year 1892 an effort was made to establish a public hospital in Atlantic City. A number of ladies and gentlemen organized what was then known as the "Atlantic City Hospital Association," and they collected a fund of about $1200. After a time most of those identified with the movement lost interest in it, and finally the fund was turned over to a private sanatorium, and applied toward the founding of a "free bed" in that institution. Through the efforts of Mayor Franklin P. Stoy, the city contracted with the institution referred to, known as the Atlantic City Sanatorium, of which J. J. Rochford was Superintendent, and for a few years all sick or injured persons, who became charges upon the city, were provided for at the Sanatorium. In this arrangement Mr. Stoy was the careful guardian of the city's interests, and to him and Mr. Rochford—the one for the city and the other for the sanatorium association—belongs the credit of providing hospital facilities in Atlantic City during the years 1894-'95-'96-'97.

The present hospital corporation had its beginning when the following notice was published in the Atlantic City morning papers of February 12, 1897 :—

HOSPITAL MEETING.

All who are interested in the hospital movement in Atlantic City are invited to meet at the Atlantic City Sanatorium this evening, at eight o'clock.

A. M. HESTON.

The following is from the hospital minutes :—

Pursuant to the above call, the following persons met at the Sanatorium this evening: A. M. Heston and J. J. Rochford. Notwithstanding the small attendance, it was decided to organize the meeting and carry out the purpose of the call.

Mr. Heston nominated Mr. Rochford as temporary president, and he was unanimously elected. Mr. Rochford nominated Mr. Heston as temporary secretary and he was unanimously elected.

On motion, it was decided to elect a board of nine governors. Mr. Heston nominated F. P. Stoy, Stewart R. McShea, M. A. Devine, John F. Hall, M. V. B. Scull, H. S. Scull and J. Leonard Baier, Jr. Mr. Rochford nominated Lewis Evans and A. M. Heston. There being no other nominees, by special request, Miss Josephine O'Brien, clerk of the Sanatorium, cast the ballot and the above-mentioned persons were declared duly elected. The secretary was directed to notify the gentlemen of their election and request them to meet at the Sanatorium on Wednesday evening, February 24, 1897, to perfect arrangements for organizing the Atlantic City Hospital Association.

Extract from minutes of February 24, 1897 :—

Resolved, That this board elect six additional members, making a board of fifteen, and a solicitor.

Mr. Stoy nominated Louis Kuehnle; Mr. H. S. Scull nominated William G. Hoopes; Mr. Heston nominated Charles Evans, H. H. Deakyne, James D. Southwick and Isaac Bacharach. They were duly elected. Allen B. Endicott was elected solicitor of the Board, to serve without salary.

The morning following the first meeting, on February 12, 1897, the papers contained an account of the meeting, written by Mr. Heston, in which those present were described as "enthusiastic, earnest," etc., but the public was kept in ignorance of the fact that but two persons were present. If the exact truth had been made known at the time, and the public understood that there had been no response to the call, the hospital cause might have remained dead, and Atlantic City, for months, at least, would have been dependent upon a private institution for the care of her sick and injured. It required a little deception to impress upon the gentlemen selected as a Board of Governors that they had been chosen at an "enthusiastic meeting," [made up of two persons], to carry on the hospital work in Atlantic City.

Subsequently, at a meeting held on April 9, 1897, the constitution and by-laws were adopted and permanent officers elected as follows : President, F. P. Stoy ; Secretary, A. M. Heston ; Treasurer, Lewis Evans.

The Women's Auxiliary was organized at the Hotel Dennis on November 27, 1897, and the money collected by the ladies, amounting to $616.71, was set aside toward the furnishing of the hospital, when built.

The hospital was incorporated under and by virtue of the provisions of an act of the legislature of New Jersey, approved March 9, 1877, and the supplements thereto. The certificate of incorporation is dated April 9, 1897. On September 9, 1897, the City Council of Atlantic City appropriated $2,500 for "Hospital Expenses," and placed this sum at the disposal of the hospital corporation. The contract which the city had made in previous years with the Atlantic City Sanatorium was renewed by the hospital corporation, on a basis of $125 per month for the maintenance of a free dispensary, and $1 per day for the board of each patient placed in the institution. It was estimated that on this basis the money appropriated by City Council would pay for the dispensary work and board of patients for a period of eight months.

On September 9, 1898, City Council made another appropriation of $4,000 for hospital purposes. The contract with the Sanatorium was continued from month to month, and on November 9, 1898 (the corporation having in the meantime purchased the property on Ohio avenue), the contract with the Sanatorium was ended.

The property on Ohio Avenue near Pacific was purchased of Henry J. White, of New York, on August 20, 1898. It consisted of a lot, 100 feet front by 175 feet in depth, with a building on the north side, containing twelve rooms. The purchase price was $16,000, on account of which the Board of Governors paid $2000 in cash, and executed a second mortgage of $6000. The property was purchased subject to a first mortgage of $8000.

Plans for alterations to the building were drawn by Architect Harold F. Adams, who made no charge for his services in preparing plans or supervising the work. The cost of the improvements to the building and grounds exceeded $3000, and to cover this the Board of Governors placed two notes of $1500 each in the Atlantic City National Bank.

Mr. Charles Evans, a member of the Board, contributed $1000, which was expended in making the original purchase from Mr. White. Other persons contributed smaller amounts and a number of friends donated

Atlantic City Hospital—Temporary Building

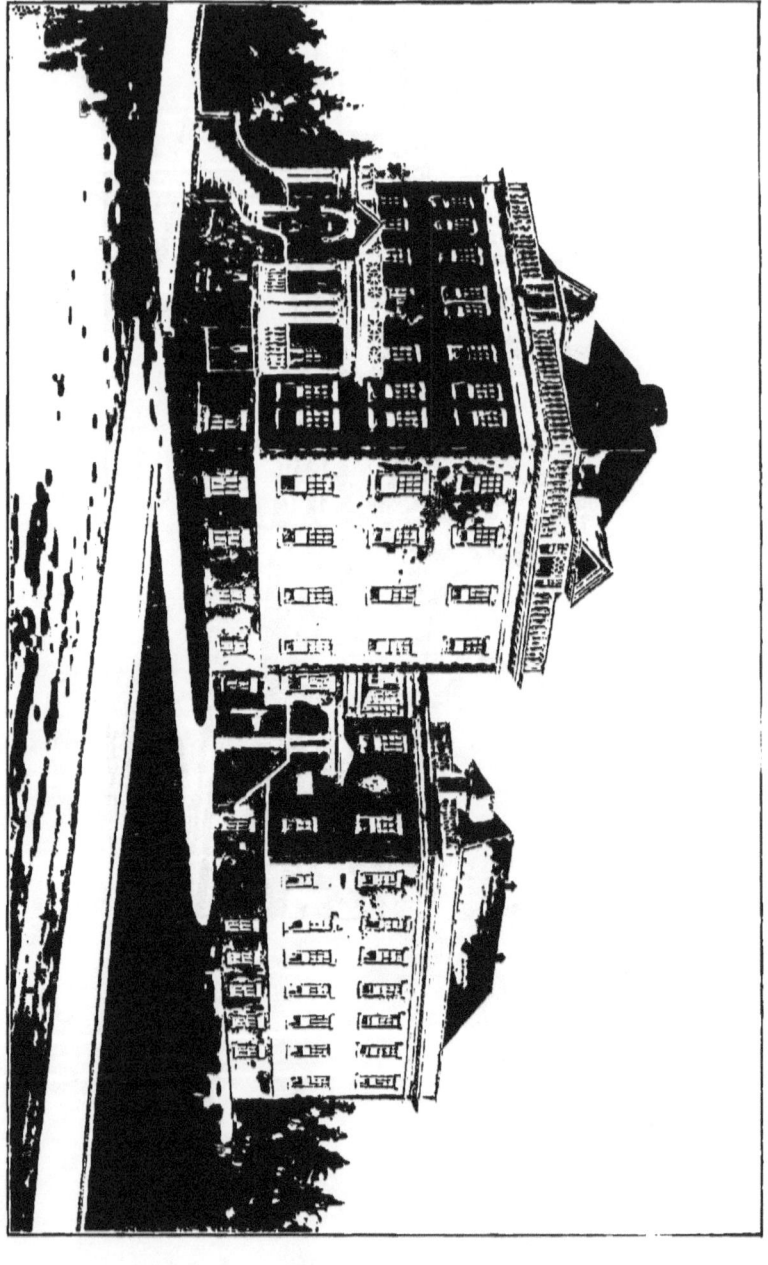

PROPOSED MAIN BUILDING

Atlantic City Hospital

BOICE ANNEX—IN COURSE OF ERECTION

articles of furniture and supplies. The furniture, in the main, was provided by the Women's Auxiliary, the Board of Governors, Mrs. R. M. Jacobs, Mrs. David Giltinan, Mrs. Max Riebenack, Mrs. S. W. Leeds, Mrs. Frederick Hemsley and Mrs. C. Retter. Each of these ladies furnished a room in the Hospital.

The formal opening of the Hospital took place on November 30, 1898, on which occasion there were many visitors and generous welcome to all friends of the institution.

The first patient was a little boy, Gussie Johann, aged eleven years, who was suffering from a broken leg. He was an occupant of one of the free beds on the third floor on the day of the opening.

The Board of Governors had previously elected Mrs. M. W. Kimmell to the position of Superintendent, and at a subsequent meeting they elected Dr. C. M. Fish the first resident physician, to serve from December 15, 1898, to July 1, 1899.

The Philadelphia Times of December 4, 1898, said:—

Perhaps the most important event of the week in Atlantic City was the formal opening of the new Atlantic City Hospital on Wednesday. The building was open for inspection all day, and thousands availed themselves of the opportunity of visiting the institution The visitors found a hospital which, while small, is thoroughly equipped and prepared to care for cases of any kind. The building is located on Ohio avenue above Pacific. It was formerly a cottage, but has been remodeled and fitted up for hospital purposes. The interior arrangement is somewhat different from that of the majority of institutions of the kind, large wards with many beds being avoided and preference given to smaller and more comfortable rooms. This is the first real hospital this city has ever had, city patients having heretofore been cared for by private contract, an arrangement that was seldom satisfactory to anyone. Last February City Controller A M. Heston took upon himself the responsibility of calling a public meeting of those interested in the hospital movement. Only two persons. Mr. Heston and J. J. Rochford, responded to the call; but an organization was affected and upon this small beginning has grown a hospital association that numbers among its members many of the most prominent residents of the city. A number of sites were inspected and the present property was purchased about three months ago. The grounds are spacious, affording plenty of room for extensions or a new building whenever the growing population of the city shall demand it. The management of the hospital is under the charge of a Board of Governors who, together with the members of a woman's auxiliary which has been organized, have been untiring in their efforts to provide the city with an institution of which it need not be ashamed. The result of their labors does them great credit. The city has agreed to make an annual appropriation to the institution, but the bulk of the work of paying for the property and maintaining the hospital rests upon the Board of Governors. They have done well thus far, and the general interest that is being taken in the project assures it of success in the future.

In the early part of April, 1899, Miss Elizabeth C. Boice, of Absecon, signified her desire to erect a brick annex to the hospital building, as a memorial to her father, Henry Boice, and her generous offer was accepted by the Board of Governors. This building is now in course of erection, and will be ready for use in the fall of 1899. The cost, when finished, will be about $7600, exclusive of the furniture. The building was designed by Architect Harold F. Adams, and is complete in all its appointments. It has both male and female wards, accommodating about twenty free patients ; also two smaller wards, one for infectious diseases and the other for children. The latter is known as the Kate M. Boice Ward, in memory of Miss Boice's deceased mother. There are also two private rooms. Miss Boice is a young lady of unusual intelligence and is deeply interested in charitable work. It is hoped that her example will induce others to give liberally to the hospital. A new executive building is needed and in a short time another building, similar to the Boice Annex, will have to be erected. To build and equip the former will require at least $15,000, and the latter will cost, approximately, $8000. The hospital is now burdened with a debt of $16,000.

Young's Pier

In their last annual report the Board of Governors say :—

The board feels that in all respects the hospital has met the expectations of its promoters. It is carefully and economically managed and is proving itself worthy of the encouragement and support of every friend of humanity. All who are interested are urged to inspect the institution on visiting days, Tuesdays and Fridays, from two to five. They will be welcomed by the matron and attendants, and can visit any of the wards, unless, for special reasons, the attending physicians have given orders to exclude visitors. Immediate relatives of patients will be admitted on other days, by permission of the attending physicians. Clergymen will be welcomed at any time, if their visits be desired by the patients and not injurious to those upon whom they call.

Necessarily, the maintenance of such an institution involves a continuous and considerable outlay. The expenses, including interest on mortgages, are nearly $100 a week, and generous assistance is therefore needed. Surely the hospital is Atlantic City's most worthy charity—the one in which all faiths, all creeds and all conditions can co-operate. We believe that all charitably disposed persons will gladly give to this young and struggling institution the material aid that is necessary, and lift it above any urgent needs.

A public institution of this character is especially in need of liberal endowments, and we appeal to the rich to give of their abundance to the Hospital. The sum of $5,000 will endow a room, or $2,500 a bed, in perpetuity. Societies, lodges or corporations may acquire the right of occupying with their sick, one or more beds in the Hospital, for a period not exceeding nine months in any one year, by the payment of $200 for each bed ; or, for a period of twelve months, by the payment of $300 for each bed. The Eutre Nous Club, a newly organized society of young ladies have voluntarily agreed to provide for one free bed by contributing the sum of $300 annually to the hospital fund.

Country Club House.—No sooner did golf become popular in the United States than Atlantic City hastened to lay out links (the finest in America) under the patronage of "The Country Club," an organization of gentlemen of Atlantic City, which has expended much money upon its athletic grounds and club houses. The links are on the mainland, the bluff of the New Jersey coast overlooking Lake's Bay, separated from Atlantic City by a prairie of meadows five miles wide, and of unlimited length—an ideal locality for the game. The links overlook this view of green meadows and sea, while the city is but twenty minutes distant by motor car. Adjoining the links is the shore road, a beautiful highway running amid quaint little villages and fine residences. This road extends along the entire New Jersey coast from near Sandy Hook to Cape May. To the skilled golfer the grounds appeal with a fascination akin to that felt by a connoisseur in the presence of a masterpiece. A visit to the Club House and the Golf Links will appeal not only to those interested in the Club, but to those who seek the enjoyment of country club life in connection with the charms of the seashore.

Lighthouse.—The lighthouse is an object of much interest, at the northeastern end of the island, the house of the keeper facing Rhode Island Avenue. The extreme height of the tower, from base to pinnacle, is one hundred and sixty-seven feet, to outside gallery one hundred and fifty feet, and to the focus of the lamp, one hundred and fifty-nine feet. The ascent of the gallery is by two hundred and twenty-eight spiral steps. The lamp is what is known as Funk's mineral-oil lamp, with fixed white light and Fresnel lens of the first order, and from the deck of a vessel can be distinguished from other lights at a distance of nineteen miles. The lighthouse is open to visitors from nine A. M. to twelve M. in summer time, and from eleven to twelve in the winter season, Sundays and stormy days excepted.

The great number of wrecks that were continually occurring on the beach caused Dr. Jonathan R. Pitney and other gentlemen to turn their attention to the absolute necessity that existed for the erection of a lighthouse on this beach. Between 1834 and 1840, the proposal was first agitated. Notwithstanding the exertions of Dr. Pitney, the lighthouse project slept for several years. In 1853, after the railroad had been surveyed, Dr. Pitney again agitated the subject. He circulated petitions for signatures, wrote to Congressmen, and published articles in the newspapers. The result of these labors was the granting of an appropriation of thirty-five thousand dollars for a lighthouse. Thus Atlantic City has to-day one of the best lighthouses in the country, which, with later improvements, cost upwards of fifty thousand dollars. The tower of the lighthouse was first illuminated in January, 1857.

Life-Saving Station.—The Atlantic City Life-Saving Station is situated at Pacific and Vermont Avenues, and is in charge of a captain, with seven assistants. The present building was finished in December, 1884, and is one of the finest life-saving stations on the coast of the United States. It is a pretty Gothic structure, with three rooms and a pantry on the first floor and three rooms on the second. Above the roof there is a tower or lookout, where a constant watch is kept for vessels in distress. The building is open to visitors at all hours of the day, and the obliging captain, or any of his assistants, will take pleasure in explaining to any one the method of saving life and property from destruction by the fury of the elements. On the first clear day of each week the crew goes through an interesting drill with the mortar and lifeline, sea-car and surf-boat, beginning at eight o'clock in the morning.

The system of life-saving is interesting to every American visitor, because of the fact that it is considered the best organized and most efficient in the world. There are eight seamen on duty, who patrol the coast at night on the lookout for vessels in distress.

Weather Bureau.—The United States Weather Bureau in Atlantic City is situated in the Real Estate and Law Building at Atlantic and New York Avenues. This station was opened December 10, 1873, in the Government Life-Saving House, about one hundred yards from the lighthouse. Subsequently it was removed to its present location. The anemometer, wind-gauge and rain-gauge are on well exposed parts of the building. Visitors will be welcomed by the observer, who takes his observations at eight A. M. and eight P. M., and finds pleasure in explaining the methods of conducting the service.

Thoroughfare.—The Thoroughfare is a sheet of water that abounds in the finest fish, oysters, crabs and clams, and is the rendezvous of a fleet of graceful yachts, in which the visitor can cruise for pleasure or for fishing, either on the smooth waters of the inlet, or upon the briny waters of the Atlantic. Omnibuses and the electric cars will convey visitors to the wharves, where boats can be hired and fishing-tackle procured at a moderate charge.

Brigantine and Peters' Beach.—Brigantine is situated across the Inlet from Atlantic City and can be reached by ferry or sail from the Inlet wharf. Brigantine is noted for the fishing in the vicinity, while a trolley road along the beach and several pavilions contribute toward the pleasure of visitors. This beach is one of the old-time resorts for sportsmen who enjoy "roughing it." For this sort of pleasure it was one of the choicest places along the coast. Blue-fish, flounders, porgies, bass and weak-fish are caught in abundance. The adjacent meadows and marshes are alive with snipe, curlew, marlin and the whole

Seaside House

Easter Sunday, 1898, on the Boardwalk—Looking Westward

family of wading birds. Wild geese, duck, brants and teal are to be had in large quantities in season. The crabbing is exceptionally good, and the bathing is safe. The upper end of this beach was for many years the breeding place for sea gulls. Myriads of these birds would congregate there. The eggs were laid in the sand, the nest being a mere hollow, with sometimes a few twigs and leaves. The breeding time was July and August.

Casino.—The Casino is located on the Boardwalk, overlooking the sea, near the foot of Indiana Avenue. It affords various kinds of amusements for adults and all reasonable attractions for the little folks. The sun parlors are especially adapted for the use of the many invalids and convalescents who find new life in our health-giving ozone during the spring months. Adjacent to these sun parlors are the office of the Casino and the reception room, the latter supplied with massive open fire-places. Above the reception room, and reached by broad, easy steps, is the assembly room, suitably furnished with a stage used for private theatricals, readings, musicales, and similar entertainments. On all sides of the assembly room are sun parlors, reading and smoking rooms.

In the one-story extension at the rear are well lighted and well ventilated dressing rooms for surf-bathing, luxuriously furnished, hot and cold sea-water baths, and also well appointed dressing rooms for the patrons of the adjoining natatorium. This large swimming pool is built of brick, with concrete bottom and white marble sides, and is the finest on this continent. Beyond the pool are bowling alleys and shuffle-board parlors.

A broad promenade, passing through the centre of the building, connects the reception room with all of the apartments, or they may be more privately reached through an enclosed passage running along the west side of the edifice. At the end of this passage is a *porte cochere*, for the benefit and protection of those patrons of the Casino who arrive in carriages. At one side of the main building is a general mart and underneath the reception room and sun parlors is a children's playroom, where the little ones may romp and play to their heart's content.

The Casino is conducted on the club plan, but admission is by tickets, instead of introduction, and the proprietor reserves the right to exclude any one for any cause. This is done to make it as select as possible for visitors.

The subscription is 50 cents a day, or $2.50 a week. This includes admission, day and evening, to the daily concerts and to the dances, two of which are given every week. The cost of the Casino was $60,000.

Post Office.—The Post Office is located on New York Avenue below Atlantic Avenue. The letter boxes are distributed throughout the city, from which collections are made several times daily. All hotels have drop boxes in the offices where letters may be posted. Mail matter addressed to individuals, at the hotel at which they are staying, can not be obtained at the general delivery window in the post office. The regulations of the department require it to be sent to the addressed hotel. All postal business which properly belongs to a first-class office may be transacted at the city office.

Academy of the Sacred Heart.—This institution was first opened in a cottage on Conecticut Avenue in May, 1883, but in November following it was removed to its present location on Park Place, directly opposite the Disston villa. The school is conducted by the ladies of the Sacred Heart, and is an institution of which Atlantic City may well feel

Cottage of C. H. McPherson—Residence of Col. George P. Eldridge—Cottage of Thomas M. Thompson—Cottage of Mrs. Cuthbert Roberts

proud. The grounds around the villa extend to the beach, and every facility is afforded the pupils for sea-bathing and healthful exercise in the open air. The building is heated with steam, and is furnished with all the modern improvements. Both boarding and day pupils are received, and the terms may be had on application to the Superior. These ladies devote themselves, also, to the education of a large number of children in their parochial school on Ohio Avenue.

Mercer Memorial Home.—This institution, the corporate name of which is Seaside House for Invalid Women, was organized in 1878. Its object is to provide at the seashore a place where invalid women, of moderate means, can spend a few weeks and have not only the comforts of a home, but also good nursing and the care of a physician, at a price which they are able to pay, but much below the actual cost. It differs from other seaside institutions for women in that it is intended for invalids only, and in this respect it meets a want which has often been felt by those who come in contact with the masses of working-women in our large cities.

In 1884 the building at the corner of Ohio and Pacific Avenues was erected, largely through the munificence of the late Mrs. J. C. Mercer, of Philadelphia, who gave forty thousand dollars for the purpose. An addition to the east wing of the building, finished in 1894, increased its capacity about one-third. The building is one of the finest of its size in Atlantic City, and is provided with every convenience for the care of sick women. Its sanitary arrangements are as near perfect as they can be made. Besides sitting-rooms, bath-rooms, parlors, writing-room, dining-room, offices, linen-rooms, trunk-rooms, servants' rooms, and the like, there are about eighty bed-rooms, capable of accommodating over one hundred patients. These are neatly furnished, and each patient has a comfortable spring-bed, with hair mattress. There are a number of bed-rooms on the first floor, and an easy, inclined plane runs from this floor to the ground, so that those unable to walk can be wheeled from their bed-rooms to the beach.

Children's Seashore House.—This institution (the first of its kind in the United States) was opened in a small cottage in 1872. In July, 1883, it was re-opened in its present location, at the sea-end of Ohio Avenue, occupying what is now the main building. Fourteen smaller buildings have since been erected within the grounds by visitors at the different hotels, each bearing the name of the house by which it was erected. They consist of one room each, furnished with immaculate linen, cleanliness being the cardinal feature of the institution. There are now accommodations for over one hundred children and about thirty mothers. The object of the corporation is to maintain at the seashore an institution in which children of the poorer classes, suffering from non-contagious diseases, or from debility, incident to the hot weather and a crowded city, may have good nursing and medical care, without regard to creed, color or nationality. Children over three years of age are cared for by competent nurses in the large, airy wards of the main building; and those too young to be separated from their mothers, are assigned to the little cottages which have been erected for the mothers almost upon the beach. One of them is assigned to each mother with a sick infant. She may also have one other child with her, and have for herself and children the exclusive use of the cottage, taking care of it and her children, but having her meals provided for her in the main building. A separate building, located immediately on

Amidst the Breakers

the beach, is used for every serious case, needing closer attention and greater quiet than can be had otherwise.

The children are under the care of a resident physician, a corps of nurses and a matron, and the total charge, including board, washing, medical attendance, bathing, and occasionally driving or sailing, is not over three dollars per week. A number—limited by the means at the command of the managers—are received without charge. Applications for admission are made to an examining physician, who furnishes railroad tickets, provided at a reduced rate. The house is open to visitors Tuesday and Friday mornings from half-past nine to half-past ten o'clock, and every afternoon from three to five o'clock.

Somers' Point.—Somers' Point, one of the oldest ports of entry in the United States, is a favorite resort for sportsmen. It is reached by steamers from Longport, but the popular way is by railroad, across the meadows to Pleasantville, and thence to Somers' Point. The ride in pleasant weather is in open cars across the wide expanse of salt meadows and through a fertile farming country to the bay, on which Somers' Point is located. In its vicinity, many years ago, was the summer encampment of the Algonquin Indians, who enjoyed the bountiful supply of oysters and game. The charge is 25 cents for the round trip.

The Elephant.—This colossal wooden animal is situated at South Atlantic City, and is easily reached by either electric car or drive along the beach front. It was erected in 1881 at a cost of $12,000.

Fishing and Crabbing.—The fishing and crabbing grounds around Atlantic City are excellent. Goodies are caught in large numbers off the pier, while further out at sea, weak-fish, blue-fish, sea-bass, sheepshead, etc., are numerous. Yachts at the Inlet are provided with tackle for the use of passengers, and any of them can be engaged by the day or half-day. No fixed schedule of rates is arranged, the price depending entirely upon the time the party is out.

The Thoroughfare is the best grounds for crabbing, and boats for this can be hired at the drawbridge, or at the foot of California avenue, both points being accessible by 'busses. Ladies take much to this sport, the sole outfit required being an old costume, a large sun hat, a net and bait. These latter can be secured at the boat-houses.

On the west bank of the Thoroughfare there is nothing but salt marsh, which extends inland for several miles. Here the sportsman has his paradise. This marsh is well supplied with game from the middle of July until the close of winter. The summer season brings the curlew, martin, willet, yellow legs, plover, tell tales and other variety of snipe, as well as other birds. The marsh hen season opens the latter part of August. Then the small boats are in demand, and with a muscular native as a pusher the light skiff is sent close to the long grass which lines the small creeks tributary to the Thoroughfare, these being the feeding grounds of the "mud hens." During the winter the meadows offer a vantage ground for duck shooting, and large numbers of these are brought home as trophies of the day's sport.

Speedway and Other Drives.—The Speedway is a new drive, extending from Seaview to Longport. It is about seven miles long. Other drives in Atlantic City are as follows : Beach drive, at low tide, ten miles ; to Longport or Great Egg Harbor Inlet, eight miles ; the Elephant, or South Atlantic City, five miles ; Absecon Inlet and Lighthouse, two miles ; Pacific Avenue drive, five miles to Ventnor. Another pleasant drive is to the Inlet on a macademized road.

Still another ride is across the meadows to Pleasantville, and thence along the shore road to the Country Club and Somers' Point, Absecon and other pretty towns in the vicinity of Atlantic City. The road across the meadows is kept in first-class condition.

Inlet Base Ball Park.—This Park is owned by the Pennsylvania Railroad, and is used during the summer season. The grand stand seats 1000 people. The Park is reached either by electric railroad or carriage. A horse show is held at this park in the early part of the summer.

Yachting.—The boats at the Inlet are principally of the sloop and cat variety, and unless especially chartered, go for runs out to sea whenever a sufficient sized party is made up. On days when the sea is rough the trip is confined to the waters inside the bar. The boats are usually out an hour, and charge a uniform price of twenty-five cents per person. Boats can be chartered at any time for longer periods, arrangements being made with the captains.

Telegraph Offices.—The two great rival companies, the Western Union and the Postal, have main and branch offices in Atlantic City. They are also in direct connection with the cable lines. The main office of the Western Union is Atlantic and New York Avenues. The Postal main office is on Atlantic Avenue, between New York and Kentucky Avenues. Both companies maintain the district messenger service, and call boxes are to be found in every section of the city. The charge for messenger service is ten cents, but for outlying districts the charge is proportionately greater. The service is one of the best and most prompt in the State. The office, during all months of the year, are opened from six A. M. until midnight, excepting July and August, when the main offices receive and send business until one A. M.

Trolley Lines.—The trolley line on Atlantic Avenue has its terminal at the Inlet. The trolley cars travel Atlantic Avenue both ways, running southward to Sea View, a point where special and regular excursion trains land passengers. From the Inlet to Sea View the distance is three and one-half miles, fare five cents. Cars run during the summer season every two minutes, and during the other months every five minutes.

Longport, located at the opposite extremity of the island, is connected with Atlantic City by a regular schedule of trains, operated by electricity, and also in summer by open trolley cars on Atlantic Avenue. Regular cars are run from the Inlet to Longport without change. The fare is ten cents each way. The ride is a popular one with visitors.

Brigantine.—On the opposite shore of the Inlet is Brigantine Beach. It is reached by yachts and by a ferry of steamers operated by the Brigantine Transit Company. The road follows the contour of the beach to Little Egg Harbor Inlet, a distance of seven miles. The cars are double-decked and run swiftly. The road passes the treacherous Brigantine Shoals, upon which hundreds of vessels of all kinds have been wrecked, accompanied by great loss of life. The charge for the round trip is twenty-five cents.

Longport.—Longport is below Atlantic City, and occupies the western end of the island, bordering on Great Egg Harbor Inlet. Its water advantages are unique. The ocean, the inlet and the thoroughfare surge restlessly or wave pleasantly on three sides of it. The island narrows and is scarcely more than one block in width in the improved portion of Longport, rendering both bathing and fishing convenient. The ocean beach is broad, smooth and level, making a fine promenade ground when

Atlantic City High School

the tide is out and safe bathing when the tide is in. Fish are abundant in the thoroughfare, and are caught steadily from the pier and break-water, which accommodate and protect the shore at different angles.

M. S. McCullough purchased the site of Longport, some two hundred and fifty acres, of James Long, in 1882, and named the town, which he immediately laid out, in honor of the former owner. Improvements have gone on steadily. Broad streets have been made and graveled, a boardwalk has been built along the beach, railroad and telephonic communication made with Atlantic City, and a post-office established. The wharfage is good, little steamers meeting trains and making regular trips to Ocean City and Somers' Point, thus affording a through route to those places from Philadelphia. Sail-boats accommodate those who desire such recreation.

The buildings of Longport are all first-class. Temperance and sanitary restrictions in the deeds possess attractions for those who summer there. The bearing of the place is literary rather than fashionable.

Two hotels accommodate many guests and are supplied with all modern conveniences, including hot sea-water baths. The cottages are diverse in architectural design. The Bay View Club House is a substantial structure and is the headquarters of the Bay-View Club, which is composed of Philadelphia gentlemen.

Chelsea.—A few blocks below the lower limit of Atlantic City is a select suburb, called Chelsea. It is laid out on a comprehensive scale with wide streets and large lots, those fronting on Pacific Avenue being sixty feet wide, and the corner ones sixty-five feet. Restrictions embodied in the deeds require all houses to be set back a good distance from the street, and prevent them also from being crowded closely together. Only one building for dwelling-house purposes is permitted on each lot. No liquor saloon or other undesirable places are allowed in the place, and stringent regulations govern the drainage arrangements. The Camden and Atlantic Railroad has a station at Chelsea, and both the electric cars and omnibuses convey passengers to and from the city.

Ventnor.—Ventnor is still another near-by resort. It is two miles below Atlantic City, and is accessible by the motor cars to Longport. The various amusements and diversions of Atlantic City are easily accessible by train, drive or beach, while freedom from noise and perfect rest are assured by its suburban location. A large and thoroughly appointed hotel is open for guests.

Public Schools.—The public schools of Atlantic City are well-appointed and six in number, the oldest being at Pennsylvania and Arctic Avenues. The original building was removed in 1887, and a new brick building erected on the site at a cost of twenty thousand dollars. The other buildings are on Indiana avenue near Arctic, Texas Avenue and Arctic, Arctic Avenue, near New Jersey, an imposing brick and stone high-school building at the corner of Illinois and Arctic Avenues, finished in 1896, and the Chelsea school, corner Brighton and Arctic Avenues, finished in 1897. The buildings are well heated, comfortably furnished, and connected with the sewer system. It has been truly said that no more cogent reason is required to show the salubrity of the climate and the desirability of Atlantic City as an abiding place for all who esteem health a blessing than the number of children born within the island's sandy rim. According to the school census of 1899 the number of school children in Atlantic City is 4574.

Atlantis Club.—This social club of gentlemen was organized on March 4, 1899. The club house is on Illinois Avenue between Atlantic and Pacific. Atlantis is really a variation of Atlantic. It is the name of an island, of vast extent and advanced civilization, mentioned by Plato and other classical writers, the existence of which has been disputed. This island was in the Atlantic Ocean, west of the Pillars of Hercules (Gibraltar) and was the passage to other islands and another continent further westward. The power of this island was exerted against the Egyptians and Hellenes. The most famous of the Athenian exploits was the overthrow of the island of Atlantis, whose power was arrayed against the countries bordering on the Mediterranean. Athens was renowned over the whole earth, for at the peril of her own existence and when the other Hellenes had deserted her, she repelled the invaders and of her own accord gave liberty to all the nations within the Pillars of Hercules. A little while afterwards there was a great earthquake, and the warrior race of Atlantisans disappeared; the great island of Atlantis sank into the sea. The submergence of this island is the explanation of the shallows which are found in the Atlantic Ocean northwest of Africa. The story of Atlantis may embody some popular legend, and the legend may have rested on certain historical facts. Bacon wrote an allegorical romance, the scene of which was laid on the island of Atlantis.

Carnival of Atlantis.—Beginning with the post-lenten season of 1900, Atlantic City will hold an annual festival, similar to the Mardi Gras of New Orleans, which will be known as the Carnival of Atlantis. Preparations for this festival are now under way, and it is proposed to make it the grandest affair of the kind ever held in this country. The name, "Carnival of Atlantis," is taken from the fabled island in the Atlantic Ocean, and the similarity of names and other features of this and the imaginary sunken city will serve not only to awaken interest in the coming carnival, but to permit of the introduction of magnificent spectacular features.

While Mardi Gras is a name that has and can be used generally in connection with such affairs, the title of Atlantis will become linked with Atlantic City by reason of the fact that the city practically rises up out of the Atlantic, and the imaginary history of Atlantis can be splendidly reproduced here.

One of the features of the carnival will be a great pageant of scores of craft of all kinds off the city front after nightfall, and as all the boats will be beautifully illuminated the marine parade will be a beautiful spectacle. A series of street processions will also be held in connection with the carnival, and nearly every line of business in the city will be represented in some manner calculated to inspire the thousands of visitors who will flock here with a fitting idea of Atlantic City's greatness.

This festival is the outcome of a movement started by Mr. T. C. Wills, who, coming to Atlantic City for his health, and having previously directed the flower festivals at Los Angeles and San Diego, Cal., as well as the Mardi Gras at New Orleans, he saw at once that Atlantic City was the ideal place for a carnival that would surpass even the great Eastertide festival at New Orleans. His plans met the approval of the leading citizens, and they are now co-operating with him in the work of preparing for the great event of 1900.

An April Sunday on the Boardwalk

Memoranda and Ready Reference.

Amusements.—The principal places of amusement are as follows : Academy of Music, Boardwalk and New York Avenues ; Young's Pier, foot of Tennessee Avenue ; Scenic Theatre, Boardwalk and Tennessee Avenue ; Schaufler's Garden, North Carolina Avenue ; Empire Theatre, Atlantic Avenue above Kentucky ; Japanese Tea Garden, Boardwalk and Massachusetts Avenue.

Banks.—In Atlantic City there are three national banks where letters of credit may be made payable—the Atlantic City National Bank, the Second National Bank and the Union National Bank. There is also a safe Deposit and Trust Company.

Baptist Church.—This edifice was completed in July, 1882, and enlarged and improved in 1893. It is a neat structure, capable of seating about five hundred. The seats are arranged in amphitheatre style.

Carriages.—Atlantic City is abundantly supplied with carriages or hacks, for which there is a schedule of charges, as follows : Carriages with two horses, with driver, one dollar and fifty cents per hour ; carriage with two horses, without driver, two dollars per hour ; phaeton with one horse, without driver, one dollar per hour ; cart with one horse, without driver, one dollar and fifty cents per hour ; saddle horse, one dollar per hour ; carriage to or from railroad depot (one or two persons), distance one mile, fifty cents ; additional passengers, twenty-five cents ; more than a mile (one or two persons), not exceeding two miles, one dollar ; additional passengers, twenty-five cents ; omnibuses from Inlet to Sea View, along Atlantic Avenue, ten cents. In calculating distances it is customary to make twelve blocks to a mile.

Catholic Church.—St. Nicholas Roman Catholic Church was built in 1856 on Atlantic Avenue, near Tennessee. In the spring of 1887 the building was removed to its present location on Pacific Avenue, near Tennessee. Many changes and improvements were made, and it is now a large and very comfortable church edifice.

St. Mary's Church edifice, at the corner of Atlantic and Texas Avenues, was dedicated in 1897. This church was formerly known as St. Monica's, and was destroyed by fire December 2, 1896.

Death-Rate.—The death-rate among residents is less than 10 in 1,000, which is probably lower than that of any other city in the country.

In relation to the resident death-rate Dr. M. D. Youngman says : "Thirty per cent. of the number are buried either in remote parts of the State or in other States, showing that they or their friends were only temporary residents, and yet claimed residence here and intended living here while the boarding-house business paid, or while they found employment as waiters, or as long as their health was conserved. A considerable percentage of these waiters are colored, the majority being children. Colored people come here for the purpose of doing laundry work and waiting, and their children are bottle-fed and neglected. The mortality is therefore very great among them in consequence. Many of these people are of a roving disposition, and stay here part of the year and go

The Islesworth and Virginia Avenue from the Boardwalk

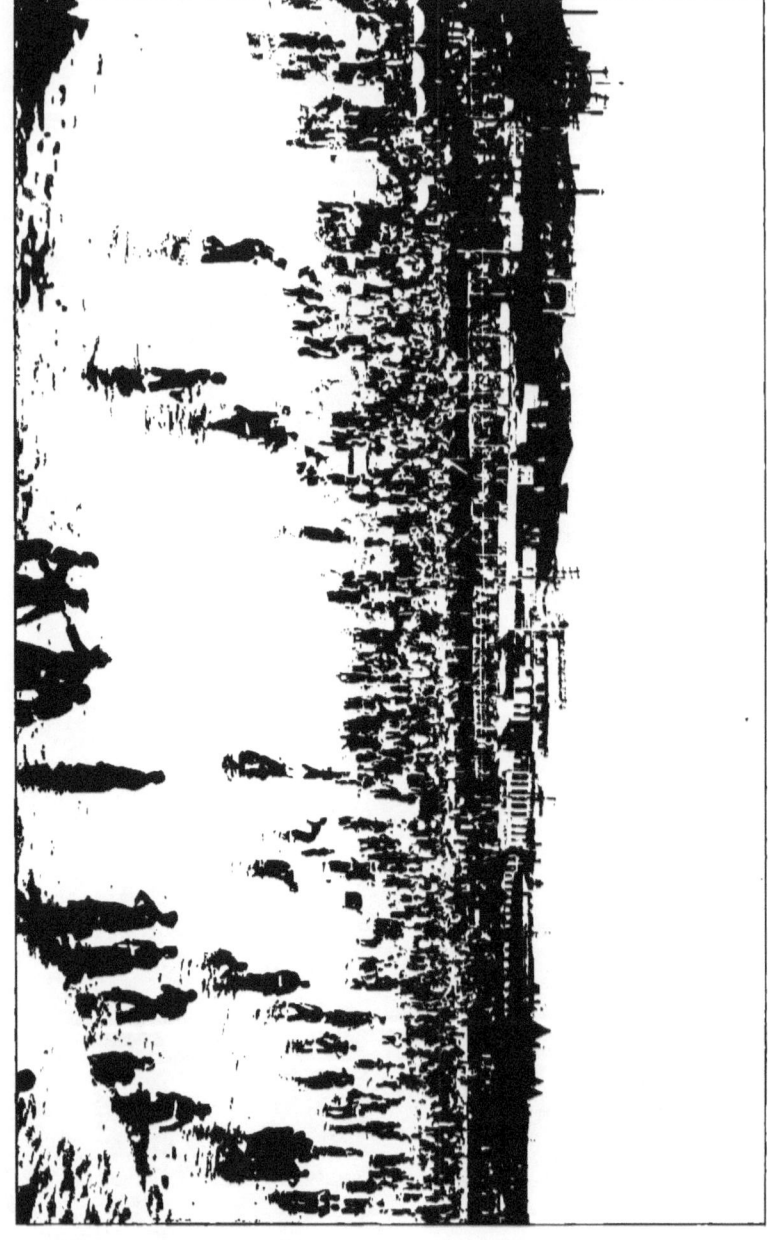

Beach and Boardwalk from Young's Pier

elsewhere the remainder, or they come and stay a year or two, and this constitutes their residence here. Many of our permanent residents are impaired lives, persons who maintain a permanency of residence here because they can not live elsewhere on account of some impairment of health. The local death-rate from acute diseases is very low. Of the non-residents the great majority are chronic invalids, many of them being in the city but a few days or even hours when they die. This is the case with children very frequently in the hot season.

Distances A-wheel from Atlantic City :—

	MILES.		MILES.
Pleasantville,	5½	Absecon,	7½
Absecon,	7½	Egg Harbor,	19
New Gretna,	21½	Elwood,	24
Tuckerton,	27½	Hammonton,	30½
West Creek,	30	Blue Anchor,	36
Barnegat,	39	Berlin,	44½
Forked River,	46	White Horse,	50
Lanoka,	48½	Gloucester,	59
Toms River,	56	Camden,	61
Lakewood,	66	Ventnor,	3½
Point Pleasant,	76	Longport,	7
Manasquan,	79	Country Club Grounds,	7
Sea Girt,	80½	Bakersville,	7½
Spring Lake,	82	Linwood,	8½
Belmar,	84	Somers' Point,	12
Asbury Park,	86½	May's Landing (River Route),	25
Deal Beach,	88¾	Oceanville,	11½
Elberon,	90½	Leeds's Point	14
Long Branch,	93	Port Republic,	16
		Manahawken,	35

Friends' Meeting-house.—This place of worship was built in 1872, previous to which the meetings of the Society of Friends were held in the school house on Pennsylvania Avenue for four consecutive summers.

Halls.—Odd Fellows' Hall, New York Avenue above Pacific; Morris Guards Hall, New York Avenue below Atlantic; Turn Verein Halle, New York Avenue below Atlantic; Memorial Hall (G. A. R.), New York Avenue above Pacific; Elks Hall, corner Atlantic and Maryland Avenues; Masonic Hall, corner Atlantic and South Carolina Avenues; Masons' Hall, corner Atlantic and Michigan Avenues.

Jewish Synagogue.—This unique building is situated on Pennsylvania Avenue above Pacific. The corner-stone was laid and the edifice completed in 1892.

Light—Gas and Electric.—Atlantic City is lighted with both gas and electricity. The Gas Works, which were completed in June, 1878, are located on Michigan Avenue near Arctic. The present capacity of the works is three hundred and fifty thousand cubic feet per day.

Connected with the Gas Works, and operated by the same company, is an electric arc-light plant, which was established in the summer of 1882. The plant furnishes light for boardwalk and avenues, besides a number of hotels and public buildings.

The city is also supplied with light from the Edison incandescent and American arc burners by the Atlantic Electric Light and Power Company, whose works are on Arctic Avenue near Kentucky.

St. Paul's M. E. Church

First Baptist Church.

First Presbyterian Church.

Lutheran Church.—St. Andrew's Evangelical Lutheran Church (English) is at the corner of Michigan and Pacific Avenues. This society was organized in June, 1887, by the Rev. William Ashmead Schaeffer, D. D., of Philadelphia. The first service was held in the upper room of a building on Atlantic Avenue above Tennessee. The congregation afterwards bought the Philopatrian Hall on New York Avenue, and changed the name to St. Andrew's Hall. In 1892 they bought the lot at Michigan and Pacific Avenues and built the present edifice thereon. The pulpit was filled by various persons until the present pastor took charge in 1894.

Methodist Church.—The first religious services held in Atlantic City were under the direction of the Methodists. The building was dedicated in 1857, and still stands where originally built, on Atlantic Avenue, below Massachusetts. It has been enlarged and improved, however, and will now seat comfortably several hundred people. Besides this, the First Methodist Church, there is the St. Paul's M. E. Church, built in 1898, the Central M. E. Church, built in 1896, Christ Methodist Protestant Church and Trinity M. P. Church.

105

Military Companies.—Joe Hooker Post, No. 32, G. A. R., meets the second and fourth Tuesday evening in each month at G. A. R. Hall.

Colonel H. H. Janeway Camp, No. 11, S. of V., meets the first and third Monday evening in each month in G. A. R. Hall.

Morris Guards, named in honor of Colonel Daniel Morris, who was one of the first residents of the place. It is both a social and a military organization, and is intended to be always ready to render any service required of a military company, and to officiate at the reception of all organizations visiting the city in a body.

Company I., attached to the Third Regiment, New Jersey National Guards.

Presbyterian Church.—There are three edifices of this denomination in Atlantic City, the principal one being at the corner of Pacific and Pennsylvania Avenues. The building was erected in 1856, enlarged some years later, and very much improved in the spring of 1887. The German Presbyterian Church was dedicated in 1884, and enlarged in 1896. The Olivet Presbyterian Church was dedicated March 27, 1898.

Protestant Episcopal Church.—St. James's P. E. Church was the first of this denomination erected in Atlantic City. It was finished in 1869, and enlarged in February, 1874. The Church of the Ascension, originally a frame building, was completed in 1879, and stood on Pacific Avenue, below Michigan, but was removed in 1886 to its present location on Kentucky Avenue, corner Pacific. The present brick edifice was completed in 1893.

Railroad Stations.—West Jersey and Seashore, South Carolina Avenue, above Atlantic.

Atlantic City (Reading System), Atlantic Avenue, between Arkansas and Missouri Avenues.

Longport and South Atlantic City, corner Tennessee and Atlantic Avenues.

Sanitation.—Atlantic City has a model system for the disposal of garbage and refuse, at the crematory. No bad odors are noticeable either in or out of the building in which the work is done, and all classes of offal and refuse, including dead animals, broken glass, and crockery ware, etc., as well as garbage, are quickly and successfully destroyed.

Sewage System.—The waves that beat on the Atlantic City beach are not required to act as scavengers for the city. Unlike other places on the coast, the surf here is absolutely free from refuse or defilement of any kind, and for this visitors are even more grateful than residents. By an underground system, which is a revelation to most city people, the air, the soil and the water are absolutely free from contamination by sewage. Briefly stated, this system, introduced by Robinson & Wallace, extensive contractors in New York City, and generally known as the West System, comprises a pumping station and reservoir, with deeply laid sewers converging to it, and filter beds situated on the salt meadows at a considerable distance from the well.

The reservoir is placed on the edge of the meadows, next that side of the city which is farthest from the ocean and the hotels. It is a walled pit, cemented inside and out, thirty feet in diameter and twenty feet deep. Connected with it is a ventilating shaft seventy-five feet high. The main sewer, which empties into the bottom of this well, is a cylindrical iron pipe twenty inches in diameter. Connected with this is a system of sub-mains and laterals of iron or glazed terra-cotta pipe.

Early Morning on the Boardwalk

Hemsley Villa—View at Pacific and Maryland Avenues

Directory of Physicians.

For the information of visitors the Publisher of the Hand Book appends
a list of practising Physicians in Atlantic City. Those
marked with a * are Homœopathists.

BALLIET, L. D.,*
    1001 Atlantic Avenue.

BARNES, W. M.,
    17 South Pennsylvania Avenue.

CROSBY, GEORGE W.,*
    716 Atlantic Avenue.

CORSON, W. A.,*
    716 Atlantic Avenue.

GARRABRANT, C.,
    Corner Atlantic and Virginia Avenues.

JOY, J. ADDISON,
    35 South Illinois Avenue.

MILLER, MARY,
    Leith Villa, Ventnor.

PENNINGTON, B. C.,
    1212 Pacific Avenue.

SOOY, WALTER C.,*
    1913 Pacific Avenue.

SOMERS, M. L.,
    2012 Pacific Avenue.

SNOWBALL, J. W.,
    1519 Pacific Avenue.

WEBSTER, J. BART,
    132 South Maryland Avenue.

YOUNGMAN, M. D.,*
    1618 Pacific Avenue.

Indiana Avenue School House. North View—Hospital for Insane,

Atlantic City Officials.

Mayor—Joseph Thompson.*

Recorder.—John S. Westcott.*

Alderman.—James D. Southwick.*

City Solicitor.—Carlton Godfrey.†

City Comptroller.—Alfred M. Heston.†

City Treasurer.—John A. Jeffries.*

City Clerk.—Emery D. Irelan.†

District Court Judge.—Robert H. Ingersoll. Appointed by Governor.

City Surveyor.—John W. Hackney.†

Tax Collector.—William Lowry, Jr.*

Mercantile Appraiser.—John W. Parsons.†

Supervisor of Streets.—Samuel B. Rose.†

Building Inspector.—Simon L. Wescoat.†

Overseer of Poor.—Daniel L. Albertson.*

City Electrician.—C. Wesley Brubaker.†

Chief of Police.—Harry C. Eldridge. ‡

Commissioner of Sinking Fund.—Alfred M. Heston. Appointed by Supreme Court of New Jersey.

City Assessors.—Stewart H. Shinn, Seraph Lillig and A. J. Withrow. Appointed by Mayor.

Chief Engineer of Fire Department.—Isaac Wiesenthal. Elected by City Council.

Members of Council.—James D. Southwick, President ; Samuel Barton, David R. Barrett, Albert Beyer, Jos. C. Clement, S. L. Doughty, Dr. J. R. Fleming, Enos F. Hann, Hugo Garnick, Wm. A. Ireland, Samuel H. Kelley, Daniel Knauer, Edward S. Lee, Henry W. Leeds, Jos. E. Lingerman, George H. Long, Edwin A. Parker.* Sergeant-at-Arms, C. S. Fort.†

Water Commissioners.—Louis Kuehnle, Dr. E. A. Reiley, Rufus Boove. Appointed by Mayor.

Superintendent of Water Department.—W. C. Hawley. Appointed by Water Commissioners.

City Hall Commissioners.—Frederick Hemsley, Charles Evans, John B. Champion. Appointed by Mayor.

City Park Commissioners.—Brinckle Gummey, Dr. A. W. Baily, Walter E. Edge. Appointed by Mayor.

Board of Health—Dr. A. W. Baily, Wm. F. Koeneke, Wm. B. Loudenslager, Arthur H. Stiles, Thomas McDevitt, Elwood S. Johnson, William Clark. Elected by City Council.

Health Inspector.—William Brode.‡

Register of Vital Statistics.—Alfred T. Glenn.‡

Board of Education.—C. J. Adams, Dr. A. D. Cuskaden, S. R. Morse, Wm. A. Bell, Aaron Hinkle, Carlton Godfrey, Paul Wootten. Elected by City Council.

Superintendent of Schools.—Dr. W. M. Pollard. ‖

Supervising Principal.—Charles B. Boyer. ‖

Principal of High School.—Henry P. Miller. ‖

Superintendent of Manual Training.—L. E. Ackerman.

Superintendent of Business Course.—F. J. Klock. ‖

---

*Elected by voters. † Elected by City Council. ‡ Life tenure. ‡ Appointed by Board of Health. ‖ Appointed by Board of Education.

111

Atlantic City Statistics.

Population of Atlantic City (Census of 1895), . .   18,329
Present population of Atlantic City, ...   24,000
Number of school children in Atlantic City in 1899, . .   · 4,574
    "   of registered voters in   "   " in 1899, ...   · 5,475
Transient population during summer season,   . .   40,000 to 150,000
Number of houses in Atlantic City, ...   · · 4,498
Number of houses built last year, ...   296
Value of Real and Personal Estate, as per assessment of 1898, $13,575,345
Actual value of Real Estate, at least,   · $40,000,000
Water Pipes laid and in use in Atlantic City, ... 48   miles.
Length of Streets, ... 51   "
Number of Public School Houses, ...   6
    "   Churches, ...   · · 21
    "   National Banks, ...   ·   3
    "   Safe Deposit Companies, . . .   1
    "   Fire Companies, . . .   · · 8
    "   Military Companies,   ·   · 4
Area of Atlantic City, ... 2,704 acres.
    "   Island between Atlantic City and South Atlantic City, 1,101   "
    "   South Atlantic City, ... 895   "
    "   Longport, ... 513   "
    "   entire Island, ... 5,213   "
Acreage of Atlantic City built upon, ... 640   "
    "   Island outside of Atlantic City built upon,   10   "
    "   entire Island built upon, 12½%, or 650   "
Distance from Inlet to lower end of Atlantic City, . . . 4½ miles.
    "   "   Atlantic City to South Atlantic City, · 3   "
    "   "   South Atlantic City to Longport, ... 1½   "
    "   "   Longport to lower point of beach, . . . 1   "
    "   "   Atlantic City to Mainland, ... 5½   "
First permanent resident on the island, Jeremiah Leeds, about   1795
First train to Atlantic City, ... July 1st, 1854
Second railroad (narrow gauge) to Atlantic City, opened July 25th, 1877
    "   "   changed to broad gauge, . . . October 5th, 1884
Double track of Reading road first used in   . . . . . April, 1889
Third railroad to Atlantic City, opened . . . . June 16th, 1880
First train on Pennsylvania system via Delaware River
    Bridge to Atlantic City, ... April 19th, 1896
Length of entire Island, ... 10 miles.
    "   Young's Pier, ... 2,800 feet.
    "   Iron Pier, ... 1,241   "
    "   Boardwalk, ... 4 miles.
Erection of Boardwalk begun . . . . April 24th, 1896
Boardwalk dedicated to public use . . . . July 8th, 1896
Cost of Boardwalk, ... · $166,057.14
Newspapers in Atlantic City (3 daily and 6 weekly), . .   9
Number of Police Officers and Patrolmen, ... 41
    "   Life Guards, ... 28
    "   active Firemen, ... 34
Height of Lighthouse, ... 167 feet.
Distance visible at sea, ... 19 miles.
Number of Steps to Lighthouse, ... 228
Cost of Lighthouse, ... $52,187
Bricks in Lighthouse Tower, ... 598,634
Highest curb elevation in Atlantic City above mean low water, 13½ feet.
Lowest   "   "   "   "   "   "   6   "
Meadow surface in Atlantic City above mean low water, . . 4   "
Number of Arc Electric Street Lights, ... 238
Number of Gas Street Lights, ... 154

Elks Hall—Atlantic Avenue, Westward from Maryland Avenue

Hotels and Boarding-Houses in Atlantic City.

The principal hotels and boarding-places in Atlantic City are herewith tabulated, special attention being called to those whose names are printed in bold-face type, as being the very best of their class.

The rates given are for one in a room. Many houses make a lower rate for two in a room. The number of rooms, as indicated in the third column of figures, must be taken as the capacity of the house, with two or more in a room.

Some of the houses marked "All the Year" are closed during November and December.

NAME OF HOUSE.	LOCATION.	RATE PER WEEK.	RATE PER DAY.	GUEST ROOMS.	TIME OPEN.	REMARKS.
Aiglen,	Michigan ave. near Pacific,	$10 to 15	$2 to 2.50	100	All the Year.	The Aiglen is thoroughly home-like and comfortable Pleasant location and good table.
Avon Inn,		12 to 20	2.50	00	"	
Ardmore,		12.50	2	35	Spring and Summer.	
Arlington,		12 to 18	Two for $5	77	All the Year.	
Albion,		15 to 25	$2.50 to 4	200	June to September.	
Aldine,		9 to 14	2	100	May 1 to Oct. 1.	
Allen,		10 to 12	1.50 to 2	60	May 1 to Oct. 1.	
Arondale,		9 to 12	2 to 2.50	50	All the Year.	
Ariel,		7 to 12	1.50 to 2	70	"	
Arno,		10 to 15	2.00 to 2.50	00	Summer Season.	
Albermarle,		12.50 to 15	2 to 1	72	All the Year.	
Alvin,		10 to 15	2 to 2.50	35	Spring and Summer.	
Amelia,		8	1.50 to 2.50	18	Summer Season.	
Amole,		8 to 10	1.50 to 2	20	All the Year.	
Altmaier,		8 to 14	1.25	51	"	
Atlantic,		8 to 15	1.50 to 2.50	20	"	
Aquarille,		9 to 15	2 to 2.50	22	"	
Acme,		10 to 12	2 to 2.50	20	"	
Archdale,		9 to 12	1.50 to 2	18	"	
Albany,		10 to 12	2 to 2.50	35	Summer Season.	
Auburn,		8 to 15	1.50 to 2.50	35	"	
Altamont,		8 to 15	1.50 to 2.50	30	"	
Avoca,		10 to 15	1.50 to 2.00	40	All the Year.	
Amherst,		10 to 12	2 to 2.50	10	"	
Angora,		8 to 10	1.50	17	Summer Season.	
Arkansas,		8 to 15	1.50 to 2.50	25	"	
Anchorage,		12 to 18	2 to 2.50	30	All the Year.	
Altemonte,	Kentucky ave. near Beach,	10 to 18	2.50 to 3	07	All the Year.	The Altemonte is situated 100 yards from the beach and is in every way an up-to-date hotel.
Almeria,		10 to 15	1.50 to 2.50	35	All the Year.	
Antlers,		10 to 18	2 to 2.50	32	Summer Season.	

Name of House	Location	Rate per Week	Rate per Day	Guest Rooms	Time Open	Remarks
Brighton,	Indiana ave. near Beach,	$25 to 50	$3.50 to 5	210	All the Year.	The Brighton is thoroughly first-class. Spacious lawn, Casino, and amusements.
Brady,		10.00	1.50	40	Spring and Summer.	
Bouvier,			2	47	All the Year.	
Boscobel,		8 to 15	2.50 to 3	56	"	
Breakers,		10 to 20	1.50 to 3	67	"	
Biscayne,	116 S. South Carolina ave.	8 to 15	2 to 3.50	50	Spring and Summer.	The Biscayne is a popular and well-kept house. Pleasantly situated. Convenient to beach and depot.
Berkshire,		8 to 18	2 to 3	61	Summer Season.	
Baltimore,		8 to 10	1.25 to 2	27	Feb. 1 to Oct. 15.	
Bew,		European	Plan.	75	Summer Season.	
Bryn Mawr,		10 to 15	2 to 2.50	46		
Belvedere,		8 to 10	1.50 to 2	21		
Bellevue,		12 to 15	2 to 2.50	49	June 1 to Oct. 1.	
Brunswick,	Pacific, bet. N.Y. and Tenn.	10 to 15	2 to 3	65	"	The Brunswick has a delightful location, and has a liberal management.
Bristol,		8 to 12	2	22	"	
Bradley,		10 to 12	2	18	"	
Beachview,		10 to 15	2 to 2.50	20	"	
Beach Villa,		10 to 12	1.50 to 2	22	Feb. 1 to Oct. 15.	
Berkeley,		14 to 18	2.50 to 4	150	All the Year.	
Boston,		8 to 12	2	31	"	
Bingham,		8 to 12	1.50 to 2	72	"	
Beechwood,		10 to 15	1.50 to 2.50	50		
Beach,		8 to 15	1.50 to 2.50	50	April to October.	
Beverly,		8 to 15	1.50 to 2.50	20	All the Year.	
Bridgeton,		8 to 15	1.50 to 2.50	20	Summer Season.	
Brevoort,		8 to 12	1.50 to 2	40	All the Year.	
Beyer,		8 to 10	1.25 to 2	14	"	
Born,		8 to 12	1.50 to 2.50	15	May to October.	
Bowker,		10 to 15	2 to 2.50	50	Summer Season.	
Brookehurst,		8 to 15	1.50 to 2.50	33	"	
Berwick,	Kentucky ave. near Beach.	10 to 20	2 to 3	75	All the Year.	The Berwick is situated near the beach and is a desirable family house.
Chalfonte,		16 to 35	3 to 5	95	Feb. to Oct.	
Chatham,		12 to 18	2.50 to 3	38		
Craig Hall,	Ocean ave. near Beach,	12 to 21	2.50 to 3	25		Craig Hall newly furnished and plumbed throughout. Evening dinners, tables for four.
Chelsea,		20 to 35	3 to 5	100	All the Year.	
Carlsbad,		8 to 15	1.25 to 2.50	45	Summer Season.	
Central,		12 to 18	2.50 to 3	120	All the Year.	
Clifton,		7 to 10	1.50 to 2	40	"	
Chester Inn,	New York ave. near Beach.	10 to 15	2 to 2.50	60	Summer Season.	The Chester Inn is pleasantly situated. Large airy bed-rooms. Accommodations the best.
Continental,		10 to 15	1.50 to 2	20	Summer Season.	

Pacific Avenue Eastward from States Avenue—Yachtmen's Pier and Pavilion

Name of House.	Location.	Rate per Week.	Rate per Day.	Guest Rooms	Time Open.	Remarks.
Cornell Inn,	. . . .	$10 to 15	$2 to 2.50	50	All the Year.	
Cedarcroft,	S. Carolina ave, near Beach	12 to 20	2 to 3.50	72	All the Year.	The Cedarcroft is a popular house. Moderate rates. Good table. Comfortable bed-rooms.
Carlton,	. . . .	10.00	2	20	" "	The Canfield is a well-kept house. Fine location. Every home comfort.
Canfield,	Virginia ave. near Beach,	10 to 15	2 to 2.50	26	" "	
Chelten,	. . . .	10 to 15	1.50 to 2	30	" "	
Colonial,	. . . .	15 to 18	2.50	42	Spring and Summer.	
Columbia,	. . . .	10 to 15	2.50 to 3	77	Summer Season.	
Chetwode,	. . . .	10 to 20	2.50 to 3	68	All the Year.	
Clarendon,	. . . .	8 to 15	2 to 2.50	60	" "	
Cleaver,	. . . .	8 to 18	2 to 3	40	" "	
Cresson,	. . . .	8 to 12	1.50 to 2	20	" "	
Congress Hall,	. . . .	10 to 25	2 to 3	220	Summer Season.	
Chelsea Haven,	. . . .	10 to 15	2 to 2.50	37	All the Year.	
California,	. . . .	8 to 15	1 to 2	25	Summer Season.	
Carisbrooke Inn	. . . .			125	June to October.	
Crescent,	. . . .	10 to 12	2 to 2.50	25	April to October.	
Camblos,	. . . .		?	35	All the Year.	
Cloud,	. . . .	8 to 12	1.50 to 2.50	35	" "	
Carrollton,	. . . .	8 to 10	1.50 to 2	31	Summer Season.	
Dennis,	. . . .	18 to 30	3.50 to 5	249	All the Year.	
Dudley Arms,	. . . .	12 to 15	2.50	40	Summer Season.	
Delaware City,	. . . .	10 to 15	1.50 to 2.50	50	Summer Season.	
Del Coronado,	. . . .	10 to 14	2	25	All the Year.	
Dartington,	. . . .	10 to 12	2 to 2.50	37	Summer Season.	
Del Monte,	Ocean end Tennessee ave.	10 to 15	1.50 to 2.50	15	All the Year.	The Del Monte is centrally located near the beach, and is under excellent management.
De Ville,	. . . .	10 to 15	2 to 3	54	Spring and Summer.	
Delaware,	. . . .	8 to 10	1.50 to 2	19	Summer Season.	
Drexel,	New York ave. near Beach,	8 to 15	1.25 to 2.50	16	May to October.	The Drexel is home-like and cheerful. Located near the beach and all places of interest.
Duffington,	. . . .	10 to 15	2 to 3	50	April to October.	
Duclou,	. . . .	8 to 12	1.50 to 2	40	Summer Season.	
Eden Vale,	. . . .	8 to 10	1.50 to 2	18	Spring and Summer.	
Edison,	Michigan ave. bel. Pacific,	10 to 16	2 to 3	60	All the Year.	The Edison is a desirable house. Nicely furnished and thoroughly comfortable. Moderate rates.
Elberone,	. . . .	8 to 12	1.50 to 2	75	" "	
Edgewater,	New York ave. near Beach,	10 to 12	1.50 to 2	24	Summer.	The Esmond is comfortable and home-like. Fine location. First-class in every respect.
Esmond,	New York ave. near Beach,	10 to 12	1.50 to 2	100	All the Year.	
Ethlyn,	. . . .	7 to 12	1.50 to 2	40	All the Year.	
Emmet,	. . . .	10 to 12	1.50 to 2.50	26		
Elsinore,	. . . .	8 to 10	1.50 to 2.50	20		
Enderby,	. . . .	8 to 12	2 to 2.50	17		

115

Name of House.	Location.	Rate per Week.	Rate per Day.	Guest Rooms.	Time Open.	Remarks.
Earley,		$7 to 9	$1.25 to 1.50	23		
Evers,		8 to 10	1.50 to 2	50		
Evard,		9 to 12	2	36		
Edna,		8 to 10	2	11		
Easthourne,		15 to 20	3 to 4	15	All the Year.	
Flynn,	14 S. Ohio ave.	8 to 12	1.25 to 1.50	10	" "	The Flynn Cottage is a good family house within easy access of the beach and all places of interest.
Fredonia,		8 to 10	1.50 to 2.50	40	Summer Season.	
Farragut,		10 to 12	2.50	60		
Florida,		10 to 15	2 to 2.50	52		
Fortescue,		12 to 17	2 to 3	24	Spring and Summer.	
Fifth Avenue,		10 to 12	2 to 3	10	Summer Season.	
Fassio,	Arctic and S. Carolina.	7 to 10	1 00 to 1.50	67	All the Year.	The Fassio is an up-to-date house.
Glasslynn,		12 to 18	2.50 to 3	40	All the Year.	
Galen Hall,		12 to 20	2 to 3	175	" "	
Garden,		25 to 50	4 to 5	30	" "	
Glenville,		8 to 12	2 to 2 50	50	" "	
Girard,		8 to 10	1.50 to 2	20	" "	
Grand Union,		10 to 12	2 to 2.50	36	" "	
Genessee,		10 to 15	1.50	20	" "	
Gilberta,	Ocean ave. near Beach.	8 to 12	1.50 to 2	23	Summer Season.	The Gilberta has a delightful location near the beach and is a good family house.
Genova,		8 to 12	2 to 2.50	200	" "	
Grand Atlantic,		10 to 20	1.50 to 2	27	Summer Season.	
Glendale,		8 to 12	1.50 to 2	19	" "	
Gloucester,		8 to 10	1.50 to 2	17	" "	
Gregson,		8 to 12	1.50 to 2	15	All the Year.	
Hathorn,		18 to 30	1 to 5	200	" "	
Haddon Hall,		12 to 18	2 to 2.50	75	" "	
Holmhurst,		10 to 15	1.50 to 2	50	Summer Season.	
Hygeia,		8 to 10	2 to 2.50	48	All the Year.	
Harmony,		12 to 15	2 to 2.50	92	" "	
Heckler,	Atlantic and Pennsylvania.	8 to 15	1.50 to 2	32		The Heckler is well kept and popular. Table and service good.
Hudson Hall,		European	2 to 2.50	26		
Howard,	Tennessee ave. near Beach.	8 to 15	2 to 3	20		The Howard is a pleasant, home-like house. Thorough management. Good table.
Howell Inn,		8 to 10	2 to 1	20	June to October.	The Holland House, by the Breakers, is an up-to-date hotel. Artesian water, electric lights, etc. Meals served at any hour à la carte.
Holland,	Brigantine.	15 to 35	3 to 5	50	Spring and Summer.	
Holmes,		8 to 10	1.50 to 2	27	April to October.	
Husted,		8 to 10	1.50 to 2	50	Summer Season.	
Hazel Glen,		8 to 10	1.50 to 2	17		
Havelow,		8 to 10	1.50 to 2	21	All the Year.	

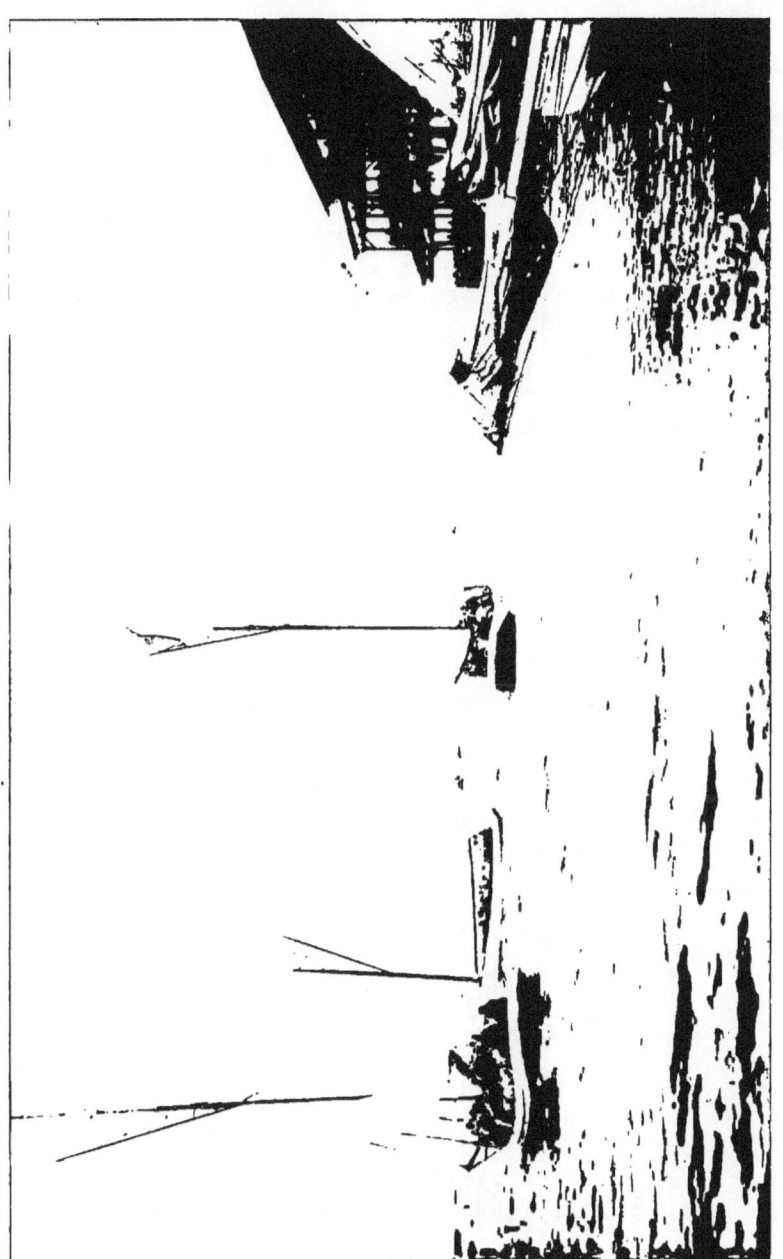

An Afternoon Sail—Starting from the Inlet

NAME OF HOUSE.	LOCATION.	RATE PER WEEK.	RATE PER DAY.	GUEST ROOMS.	TIME OPEN.	REMARKS.
Harlem	Sea end of Virginia ave.	$8 to 10	$1.50 to 2	17	All the Year.	
Islesworth	Sea end of Virginia ave.	18 to 35	3 to 5	229	"	The Islesworth has a first-class table, superior service, steam heat, every modern appointment. Salt and Fresh baths in all rooms.
Ivan Villa		8 to 12	1.25 to 1.50	11	"	
Idylwild		8 to 12	1.50 to 2	11	"	
Iroquois	S. Carolina ave. near Beach	12.50 to 25	2.50 to 3	200	"	The Iroquois is in every respect an up-to-date hotel. Best service. Steam heat. Baths, etc.
Imperial		10 to 18	2 to 3	100	"	
Isabel Villa	715 and 717 Pacific	10 to 18	2.50 to 3.50	20	"	The Isabel Villa has a most charming location. Wide porches. Ocean view. Cuisine the best.
Idaho		8 to 12	1.50 to 2	16	"	
Inlet Pavilion	Maine and Caspian aves.	8 to 12	1.50 to 2	24	Spring and Summer.	The Inlet Pavilion is a very pleasant place to enjoy good music, refreshments, and ozone.
Irvington		15 to 20	2.50 to 3	70	Feb. to Sept.	
Juniata		8 to 12	1.50 to 2	26	All the Year.	
Janson	New York ave. near Beach	8 to 12	1.50 to 2	17	"	The Janson is delightfully situated near the beach and is under excellent management.
Kentucky	Ocean end Tennessee ave.	8 to 12	1.50 to 2	40	March to October.	
Kenderton		10 to 18	2 to 2.50	60	March to October.	The Kenderton is delightfully situated, and is in every way a desirable family house.
Kenilworth		12 to 15	2 to 3	60	All the Year.	
Kenilworth Cot		12.50 to 15	2 to 2.50	25	"	
Kingston		8 to 10	1.50 to 2	30	"	
Kuehnle	S. Car. and Atlantic aves.	12 to 16	2 to 2.50	40	"	The Kuehnle is a very desirable house. Central location, and near P. R. R. Station.
Koopman		18 to 50	3 to 8	155	"	
Kilcourse	Arctic and Arkansas aves.	8 to 12	1.50 to 2	44	"	The Kilcourse is in every way a good house. Located near the Philadelphia & Reading depot.
Lamonte		10 to 12	2 to 2.50	20	"	
Luray	Kentucky ave. and Beach	16 to 45	3 to 5	200	All the Year.	The Luray is a very comfortable, first-class house. Excellent table and superior service. Sanitary arrangements complete.
Louella		8 to 12	1.50 to 2	18	"	
Lehman		15 to 20	2.50 to 3	80	"	
Lancaster		10 to 15	2 to 2.50	27	"	
Lansdale		10 to 14	2 to 2.50	33	"	
Liddlesdale	Kentucky ave. near Beach	8 to 12	2	21	"	The Liddlesdale is a well conducted family house. Convenient to beach and railroad station.
Linden		8 to 12	1.25 to 1.50	11	All the Year.	
Lashell		7 to 10	1.25 to 2	25	Spring and Summer.	
Leeds' Cottage	Ocean ave. near Beach	8 to 12	2 to 2.50	34	All the Year.	The Leedom is a pleasant house in a pleasant location. Good table and good service.
Leedom		8 to 12	1.75	22	Summer Season.	
Lincoln		8 to 10	1.50 to 2	12	All the Year.	
Littlepage		8 to 10	1.50	10	"	
Longinotti	Illinois and Atlantic aves.	9 to 12	2	14	Spring and Summer.	The Longinotti is on the European plan. Central location. Café attached.
Lenox		10 to 12	2	18	All the Year.	
Leclede		10 to 12	2	21	April 1 to October 1.	
Lamartine	Connec't and Oriental aves.	9 to 15	1.50 to 2.50	26	Spring and Summer.	The Lamartine has a delightful location. Moderate rates and good table.
Lakewood		8 to 15	2 to 2.50	36	Spring and Summer.	

NAME OF HOUSE.	LOCATION.	RATE PER WEEK.	RATE PER DAY.	GUEST ROOMS	TIME OPEN.	REMARKS.
Lelande,		$13 to 18	$2.50 to 3	100	Spring and Summer.	
Little Brighton.		10 to 20	2 to 3	47	All the Year.	
La Fontaine.		10 to 15	2 to 2.50	58	"	
Lafayette,		8 to 10	1.50	17	June to September.	
Linderman.		10 to 12	2 to 2.50	27	Summer Season.	
Lola,		8 to 10	2	32	Spring and Summer.	
Le Champlane,		15 to 25	3	80	All the Year.	
La Croix,		8 to 10	2	18	Summer Season.	
Lucerne,		8 to 10	1.50 to 2	35	Spring and Summer.	
Layton,		10 to 12	1.50 to 2	20	"	
La Belle Inn,	S. Carolina ave. near Beach,	8 to 15	1.50 to 2.50	65	April to November.	The La Belle Inn is a well-managed and desirable house. The rooms are pleasant and the table good.
Loraine,		18 to 21	1 to 3.50	80	All the Year.	
Lamborn,		10 to 15	2 to 2.50	40	"	
Minerd,		12	2	30	Spring and Summer.	
Majestic,	Virginia ave. near Beach,	12 to 25	2.50 to 3.50	100	March to October.	The Majestic is a favorite house, with careful management. Excellent cuisine and service.
Mansion,		16 to 25	3 to 4	190	Summer Season.	
Malvern,		8 to 12	1.50 to 2	20	"	
Manhattan,	S. Carolina ave. near Beach,	10 to 15	2 to 2.50	74	All the Year.	The Manhattan is always popular. Near beach and central location.
Maryland,		12 to 15	2 to 2.50	51	Spring and Summer.	
Marsden,	S. Carolina ave. near Beach,	8 to 20	1.50 to 3	60	All the Year.	The Marsden is a favorite house. It is centrally located and close to the beach.
Melos,		8 to 15	2 to 2.50	24	"	
Malatesta,	Atlantic and N. Car. aves.,	10 to 21	1.50 to 3	80	Spring and Summer.	The Malatesta is a very popular house; thorough management, pleasant rooms, and superior table.
Morton,		16 to 35	3 to 5	101	April to October.	
Melrose,		9 to 12	1.50 to 2	33	All the Year.	
Metropolitan,		10 to 12	2 to 2.50	50	Spring and Summer.	
Malta,		8 to 15	1.50 to 2	35	"	
Miller,		7 to 10	1.25 to 2	75	Summer Season.	
Maltby,		10 to 15	2 to 3	70	"	
Metropole,		12 to 18	2.50 to 3	57	April to October.	
Mt. Vernon,		9 to 14	1.50 to 2.50	90	Spring and Summer.	
Madison,		7 to 10	1.25 to 1.50	33	Spring and Summer,	
Minerva,		8 to 12	2 to 2.50	42	Summer Season.	
Mascot,		8 to 10	1.50 to 2	100	All the Year.	
Mamore,		8 to 10	1.50 to 2	17	"	
Mervine,		8 to 10	1.25 to 1.50	22	"	
Magnolia,		7 to 8	1.25	20	"	
Moss,		8 to 12	1.50 to 2.50	68	"	
Norwood,	Kentucky ave. near Beach,	9 to 14	1.50 to 2.50	65	"	The Norwood's table and other accommodations are highly commended. Modern conveniences.
New England,		10 to 16	2 to 2.50	65	"	

NAME OF HOUSE.	LOCATION.	RATE PER WEEK.	RATE PER DAY.	GUEST ROOMS	TIME OPEN.	REMARKS.
New York,	. . . .	$8 to 10	$1.50 to 2	22	All the Year.	
Nuttall,	. . . .	8 to 12	1.50 to 2	20	Summer Season.	
National,	. . . .	8 to 10	1.50 to 2	23	Summer Season.	
New York Ex.,	. . . .	10 to 12	2	37	Summer Season.	
Oberon,	. . . .	6 to 12	2	31	March 1 to Nov. 1.	
Ocean Queen,	. . . .	9 to 15	2 to 3	36	Summer Season.	
Osborne,	. . . .	8 to 15	1.50 to 2.50	90	Summer Season.	
Ocean Villa,	. . . .	8 to 15	2	20	All the Year.	
Oakland,	. . . .	10 to 12	1.50 to 2	55	Summer Season.	
Ogontz,	. . . .	8 to 12	1.50 to 2	15	All the Year.	
Ocean View,	. . . .	10 to 15	2 to 2.50	17	Summer Season.	
Park Cottage,	Kentucky near Beach.	8 to 12	2	41	All the Year.	The Park Cottage is a very comfortable house. Good table and attentive service.
Preston,	. . . .	8 to 10	1.50 to 2	18	Summer Season.	
Ponce de Leon,	. . . . . .	10 to 14	1.50 to 2	17	All the Year.	
Porter Cottage,	. . . . .	12 to 15	2 to 3	100	"	
Portland,	. . . .	15 to 25	3	14	"	
Pembroke,	. . . .	7 to 12	1.50 to 2	80	Summer Season.	
Patton,	. . . .	8 to 10	1.25 to 2	37	All the Year.	
Pierrepont,	. . . .	10 to 15	2 to 2.50	36	"	
Pitney,	. . . .	8 to 10	1.25 to 1.50	40	Spring and Summer.	
Paoli,	. . . .	12 to 18	2.50 to 3	28	Spring and Summer.	
Pennhurst,	. . . .	8 to 12	1.50 to 2	100	All the Year.	
Pittsburgh,	. . . .	8 to 12	2	9	"	
Presser,	. . . .	8 to 12	1.50 to 2.50	21	"	
Philadelphia,	. . . . . .	10 to 15	2 to 2.50	32	June to October.	
Pavonia,	. . . .	8 to 10	2 to 2.50	39	Summer Season.	
Quaker City,	. . . . . .	10 to 15	2 to 3	22	All the Year.	
Richmond,	. . . .	8 to 12	2	50	"	
Roxborough,	. . . . . .	18 to 25	3 to 5	12	"	
Rynear,	. . . .	12 to 18	2.50	110	"	
Revere,	Park Place, near Beach.	10 to 12	2 to 2.50	40	Spring and Summer.	The Revere has a very desirable location, good table and good service. Popular the year round.
Renova,	. . . .	12 to 16	2 to 2.50	32	All the Year.	
Raymond,	. . . .	12 to 15	2	55	"	
Rutherford,	. . . .	12 to 18	2.50 to 4	16	"	
Runnymede,	. . . .	17 to 30	2.50	70	Summer Season.	
Roman,	Ocean end St. Charles Place	Eurp. and Am. Plan.	Am. Plan.	60	All the Year.	The Roman has large rooms; select neighborhood; first-class cuisine. Café attached.
Radnor,	. . . .	6 to 10	1.50 to 2	10	"	

Name of House.	Location.	Rate per Week.	Rate per Day.	Guest Rooms.	Time Open.	Remarks.
Royal,		$8 to 12	$1.50 to 2	101	All the Year.	
Rossmore,	Tennessee ave. near Beach.	10 to 15	2 to 2.50	51	" "	The Rossmore is near the beach and churches. No liquors. Family trade specially.
Roanoke,		10 to 18	2.50 to 3	66	" "	
Reading,		8 to 10	1.50 to 2	17	Spring and Summer.	
Ruscombe,		9 to 12	1.50 to 2	60	All the Year.	
Rudolf,	Ocean end of New Jersey.	18 to 30	1 to 5	200	All the Year.	The Rudolf is a refined and luxurious house. Table and service unexcelled.
Ramsgate,		8 to 10	1.50 to 2	19	" "	
Robbins,		8 to 12	1.50 to 2	20	" "	
Ryan Cottage,		7 to 10	1	40		
Seaward,	1102 Pacific ave. ab. Tenn.	9 to 12	1.50 to 2	15	All the Year,	The Seaward is home-like and comfortable. Convenient to beach and station. Good table.
Sandhurst,		12 to 20	2.50 to 3	100	" "	
Southwick,		8 to 12	1.50 to 2.50	12	" "	
Sterling,		10 to 12	1.50 to 2	11	" "	
San Marcos,	Pacific ave. above Conn.	14 to 18	2.50 to 3	90	" "	
Sunset,		8 to 10	1.50	16	Summer Season.	
Shelburne,	Michigan ave. and Beach.	18 to 40	3 to 4	90	All the Year.	The Shelburne is a refined and luxurious house. Every convenience. Table and service unsurpassed. Unrivaled ocean view.
Seabright,		15 to 20	2	50	Spring and Summer.	
St. Elmo,		8 to 10	1.50 to 2	11	All the Year.	
Seaside,	Penna. ave. and Beach.	16 to 25	1 to 4	112	Summer Season.	The Seaside is a first-class house. Delightfully situated, overlooking the sea. Excellent table and service. Every modern convenience. Daily
Somerset,		8 to 12	1.50 to 2	121	Summer Season.	
Senate,		16 to 24	3	125	Spring and Summer.	
Schaufler's,	Atlantic and N. Car aves.	16	2.50	100	All the Year.	Schaufler's has a summer garden attached. Daily concerts in summer-time.
Staiger,		10 to 15	2 to 2.50	50	" "	
Stanton,		10 to 12	1.50 to 2	15	" "	
Stanley,		10 to 15	1.50 to 2	75	" "	
St. Charles,	Foot of St. Charles Place.	18 to 30	3 to 5	200	Summer Season.	The St. Charles is an entirely new house. It is elegantly appointed and strictly first-class. Table and service unexcelled. Café attached.
Sea View,		10 to 15	2	40	Summer Season.	
St. Nicholas,		8 to 12	1.50 to 2	18	All the Year.	
Scarborough,		15 to 25	3	100	" "	
Strath-haven.		10 to 15	2 to 2.50	50	Spring and Summer.	
Stratford.		European.	1 to 3	100	" "	
Strand.		12 to 20	2.50 to 1.50	100	All the Year.	
Saratoga,		8 to 10	1.50 to 2	17	All the Year.	
Sunnyside,		8 to 10	1.50	16	Summer Season.	
Surf Villa,		12 to 15	1 to 2.50	35	Feb. to Nov.	
Stickney,	Kentucky ave. near Beach.	8 to 12	2 to 2.50	60	All the Year.	The Stickney is a comfortable, home-like house. Good table and good management. Always popular.
Speidel,		8 to 10	1.50 to 2	25	Summer Season.	
Spring Haven.		8 to 10	1.50 to 2	26	Summer Season.	
Sherman,		8 to 12	1.50 to 2	15	All the Year.	

Bathing Scene in August

Name of House.	Location.	Rate per Week.	Rate per Day.	Guest Rooms.	Time Open.	Remarks.
St. George.		$10 to 12	$1.50 to 2	33	All the Year.	
Shackamaxon.		8 to 15	1.50 to 2.50	30	Summer Season.	
San Antonio.		15 to 18	2.50 to 3	20	All the Year.	
Seidel.		8 to 12	1.50 to 2	48	Summer Season.	
Tacoma.		8 to 10	1.50 to 2	40	All the Year.	
Traymore.	Illinois ave. and Beach.	18 to 25	1.50 to 5	250		The Traymore is an imposing home. Large guest-rooms. Every convenience. Unsurpassed cuisine.
Temple.		8 to 10	1.50 to 2	15	Summer Season.	
United States.		13 to 30	3 to 5	200	Spring and Summer.	
Victoria.	S. Carolina ave. near Beach.	10 to 18	2 to 2.50	75	All the Year.	The Victoria's services and other features are commended. Hot and cold baths attached.
Vendome.		10 to 18	2.50 to 3	84	April to Nov.	The Van Horn Inn is a good family house. Convenient to beach and all places of interest.
Van Horn Inn.	S. Carolina ave. near Beach	10 to 18	2 to 2.50	30	Spring and Summer.	
Valdemar.		10 to 20	2 to 3	40	..	
Virginia.		10 to 15	1.50 to 2	21	..	
Vista.	Kentucky ave. near Beach.	10 to 15	1.50 to 2	35	All the Year.	The Vista is centrally located near the beach, and is a good family house.
Waverly.		6 to 15	1.50 to 2	18	Summer Season.	
Waymworth.		8 to 10	2 to 3	21	All the Year.	
Wellington.		10 to 18	2	93	..	
Wiltshire.	Ocean end Virginia ave.	10 to 18	2.50 to 3	80	March 1 to Oct. 1.	The Wiltshire is centrally located. Near ocean and new Steel Pier. Table and service unexcelled.
Wharton.		10 to 25	1.50 to 5	150	Spring and Summer	
Wetherell.		8 to 10	2 to 2.50	44	All the Year.	
Walton.	Ocean ave. near Beach.	8 to 15	1.50 to 2	55	..	The Walton is a favorite house. It is centrally located and close to the beach.
Waldorf Astoria		21 to 70	3 to 10	211	..	
West Jersey.		6 to 10	1.25 to 2	20	..	
Whittier.	Virginia ave. near Beach.	10 to 15	2 to 2.50	28	..	
Westminister.		10 to 15	2.50 to 3	60	..	
Wavelet.		9 to 10	1.25 to 1.50	19	..	
Windsor.		8 to 30	3.50 to 4	145	Feb. to Oct.	
Wilmington.		8 to 10	1.90 to 2	16	Summer Season.	
Wingfield.		10 to 15	1.50 to 2.50	15	All the Year.	
Walbridge.		8 to 10	1.50 to 2	16	Summer Season.	
Wallingford.		10 to 12	1.50 to 2.50	30	All the Year.	
Warren.		8 to 12	1.50 to 2.50	17	..	
Wentworth.		10 to 15	2	14	Summer Season.	
Wyoming.		8 to 12	1.50 to 2	50	..	
Worthington.		7 to 8	1 to 1.50	40	..	
Waldorf.		10 to 15	2 to 3	35	..	
Watkins.		8 to 12	1.50 to 2	35	All the Year.	

Physicians, Lawyers and Tradesmen in Atlantic City.

Name.	Business.	Location.	Remarks.
Adams, Harold F.,	Architect,	Real Estate and Law Building,	Designer of some of the finest buildings in Atlantic City.
Adams, I. G. & Co.,	Real Estate and Insurance,	Real Estate and Law Building,	Largest fire insurance agency in New Jersey.
Albertson & Young Co.,	Plumbers and Hardware,	2025 Atlantic ave.,	Builders' supplies, stoves, steam and hot water heating.
Atlantic City Carpet Clean'g Co	Carpets Cleaned by Steam,	1822 Baltic ave.,	Carpets cleaned from 2 to 4 cents a yard.
Atlantic City National Bank,	Banking,	Atlantic and N. Carolina aves.,	Oldest bank in Atlantic City. Capital and surplus, $170,000
Austin, W. B.,	Butcher,	New York and Pacific aves.,	Meats and provisions.
Barnes, Wm. M.,	Physician,	17 S. Pennsylvania ave.,	
Bates & Co.,	Jewelers,	926 Atlantic ave.,	Silversmiths and practical jewelers.
Bickel, Samuel D.,	Druggist,	Atlantic and Illinois aves.,	Drugs, perfumery and toilet articles.
Bolte, H. N.,	Jeweler,	912 Atlantic ave.,	Practical watchmaker and jeweler.
Bartlett, J. H. & Son,	Real Estate and Insurance,	110 South Carolina ave.,	Conveyancing, fire and life insurance.
Bruckmann, V. C.,	Real Estate and Insurance,	600 Atlantic ave.,	Property for sale, rent or exchange.
Bacharach & Sons,	Hatters and Furnishers,	1034 and 1500 Atlantic ave.,	Tailors, and men's outfitters.
Beil & Gorman,	Furniture and Carpets,	Tennessee and Atlantic aves.,	Largest furniture and carpet warehouse in South Jersey.
Balliet, L. D.,	Physician,	1001 Atlantic ave.,	
Beaumont, W.,	Carpenter and Builder,	12 S. Tennessee ave.,	Handwood finishing a specialty.
Brownley, C. J.,	Druggist,	New York and Pacific aves.,	Prescriptions, drugs and toilet articles.
Chapman, F. A.	Electrician,	1009 Atlantic ave.,	Electrical work of all kinds.
Channell Bros.,	Grocers,	1202 Atlantic ave.,	Fine and staple groceries. Low prices.
Clark, J. C.,	Dry Goods and Notions,	813 Atlantic ave.,	Large assortment. Prices right.
Cook, E. H. & Co.,	Real Estate and Insurance,	8 States ave.,	Houses for sale and to rent.
Cox, H. T.,	Harnessmaker,	2013 Atlantic ave.,	Horse clothing, harness and stable goods.
Cramer, J. P. & Co.,	Real Estate Agents,	1709 Atlantic ave.,	Insurance and conveyancing.
Crosby & Corson,	Physicians,	9 South Kentucky ave.,	
Crandall, J. F.,	Dentist,	716 Atlantic ave.,	
Cuskaden, A. D.,	Druggist,	Union National Bank Building,	
Devine & Wooton,	Real Estate and Insurance,	Atlantic and Michigan aves.,	Desirable properties for sale or rent. A wide-awake firm
Dickerson, T. J. & Co.,	Hatters and Furnishers,	1130 to 1134 Atlantic ave.,	Finest store in Atlantic City. Fine goods at low prices.
Edge, Walter E.,	Editor and Publisher,	Mensing Building,	Editor and publisher of the Atlantic City *Daily Press*.
Endicott, A. R.,	Counsellor-at-law,	Union National Bank Building,	President Union National Bank.
Edwards, D. B.,	Florist,	107 South Carolina ave.,	Beautiful foliage and bedding plants. Fresh cut flowers.
Freeman, L. E.,	Plumber,	1022 Atlantic ave.,	Steam and gas fitting. Sanitary plumbing and drainage.
Fitton, Henry,	Jeweler,	1709 Atlantic ave.,	Watches and jewelry. Repairing a specialty.
Felker, George C.,	Painter,	9 South Kentucky ave.,	House and sign painter. Superior workmanship.
Garrabrant, C.,	Physician,	1001 Atlantic ave.,	
Genenotzky, W.,	Baker,	127 North Indiana ave.,	Vienna rolls and rye bread.
Giltinan, David,	Real Estate and Insurance,	1302 Atlantic ave.,	Desirable properties for rent and for sale.

Yachting, Promenading and Bathing

NAME.	BUSINESS.	LOCATION.	REMARKS.
Girard Market,	Meats and Provisions,	2007 Atlantic ave.,	Meats, game, poultry, butter, eggs and vegetables.
Godfrey & Godfrey,	Attorneys-at-Law,	Real Estate and Law Building,	Prominent attorneys.
Goldman, T.,	Wines and Liquors,	1406 Atlantic ave.,	Choice goods for family use.
Hinkle & McDevitt,	Plumbing and Hardware,	817 Atlantic ave.,	Hot water and steam heating. Builders' supplies.
Hirsch, A.,	Cloth,	1603-05 Atlantic ave.,	Clothing and gents' furnishing goods.
Hall, John F.,	Editor and Publisher,	Atlantic ave., above Illinois.	Editor and proprietor of *Daily Union* and *Atlantic Times*
Heston, A. M.	Publisher,	14 States ave.,	Publisher *Heston's Hand-Book* and *Outing by the Sea.*
Ingram, J. G.	Druggist,	1619-21 Atlantic ave.,	Drugs, perfumery and toilet articles, prescriptions.
Irvin, Thompson,	Dry Goods,	35 South Illinois ave.,	Leading dry goods house. Large stock and low prices.
Joy, J. Addison,	Physician,		
Kessler, Gustav,	Butcher,	1913 Atlantic ave.,	Market supplies of all kinds.
Keates, William H.,	Real Estate Agent,	1212 Atlantic ave.,	Desirable cottages and hotels.
Keeler, Chas. E.,	Druggist,	Boardwalk and Kentucky aves.,	Prescriptions, drugs, perfumery, toilet articles.
Lewis, W. R.,	Grocer,	916 Atlantic ave.,	Butter, eggs, and poultry a specialty.
McGuire, E. A.,	Ship Chandlery and Hardware,	827 Atlantic ave.,	Fishing tackle and sportsmen's goods of all kinds.
Miller, Mary,		Ventnor,	
Mitchell, John W.,	Advertising Agent,	26 North Virginia ave.,	Advertisements inserted in Hand Book and newspapers.
Myers' Union Market,	Butchers,	1513 Atlantic ave.,	A leading market house. Chicago tenderloins a specialty.
Myers, Fred.,	Baker,	1511 Atlantic ave.,	Columbian Bakery. Superior bread, pies, and cakes.
McLaughlin, William.	Editor and Publisher,	1216 Atlantic ave.,	Editor and proprietor of the *Sunday Gazette.*
McAllister, R.,	Coal,	Baltic and Kentucky aves.,	Superior coal; full weight; promptness.
Nassano Bros.,	Fruit Dealer,	1210 Atlantic ave.,	Choice fruits, nuts, and confectionery.
Pennington, B. C.,	Physician,	1212 Pacific ave.,	
Powell, William M.,	Physician,	16 South Indiana ave.,	
Packard, E. M.,	Dentist,	Penna. and Atlantic aves.,	
Phillips, A. H. & Co.,	Insurance and Real Estate,	1115 Atlantic ave.,	Agents for a number of first-class companies.
Raith, C. C.	Dentist,	New York and Atlantic aves.,	
Reed, John C.,	Real Estate and Law,	11 S. New York ave.,	
Ridgway, Wm. F.,	Druggist,	Atlantic and Penna. aves.,	Compounding of prescriptions a specialty.
Reynolds, Walter,	Physician,	1322 Pacific ave.,	
Ritter, Neilson J.,	Real Estate,	Union Bank Building,	Real estate, insurance and mortgages.
Rice, E. T.,	Millinery and Fancy Goods,	9 S. New York ave.,	All the latest novelties in ladies goods.
Roesch & Sons,	Butchers,	Maryland and Atlantic aves.,	Market supplies of all kinds.
Rotholz, Samuel,	Clothier,	1210 Atlantic ave.,	Men's outfitter. Hats and furnishing goods
Rosenbaum, Jacob,	Auctioneer,	Maryland ave. below Atlantic,	
Sabath, W.,	Family Liquors,	1608 Atlantic ave.,	Imported and domestic wines and liquors.
Schultz, Herman,	Barber,	924 Atlantic ave.,	
Somers, M. L.,	Physician,	2012 Pacific ave.,	
Seifert, D. I.,	Jeweler,	920 Atlantic ave.,	Practical watchmaker and jeweler for 12 years.
Shinn, C. C.,	Real Estate Agent,	Real Estate and Law Building,	Insurance, conveyancing and mortgage loans.

NAME.	BUSINESS.	LOCATION.	REMARKS.
Stadler, F.,	Confectioner and Baker,	Atlantic and Virginia aves.,	Ice cream parlors.
Sooy, Walter C.,	Physician,	1021 Pacific ave.,	
Stephany, Robert E.,	Att'y and Counselor-at-Law,	Real Estate and Law Building,	Fire insurance agency. Supreme Court practice.
Snowball, J. W.,	Physician,	1519 Pacific ave.,	
Senseman, Wilson,	Real Estate Agent,	1026 Atlantic ave.,	Conveyancing. Cottages for rent and for sale.
Shreve, John G.,	Editor and Publisher,	Atlantic ave.,	Proprietor of the Atlantic City *Daily* and *Weekly Review.*
Stout, H. A.,	Architect,	Real Estate and Law Building,	Designer of some of the finest buildings in Atlantic City.
Union National Bank,	Bankers,	Kentucky and Atlantic aves.,	Solid as a rock.
Voelker, Carl,	Editor and Publisher,	1216 Atlantic ave.,	Proprietor of the *Frie Presse.*
Wright, J. P.,	Undertaker,	33 North Virginia ave.,	Graduate of the United States College of Embalming.
Webster, J. Bart,	Physician,	112 South Maryland ave.,	
Wright's, Willard,	Druggist,	Atlantic and Virginia aves.,	Prescriptions carefully compounded.
Young, H. R.,	Real Estate Agent,	6 States ave.,	Properties for sale and to rent
Young, J. L.,	Amusements,	Boardwalk and Tennessee ave.,	Owner of Young's Ocean Pier.
Youngman, M. D.,	Physician,	1618 Pacific ave.,	

Everybody goes to Brigantine...

BY BOAT AND TROLLEY CAR

Across the Inlet   Along the Beach

Brigantine Transportation Company Steamers
run every few minutes in season

...See Holland House advertisement

MYERS' UNION MARKET

1513 ATLANTIC AVENUE

The leading house for the sale of all kinds of
meats and country produce

Fresh and Salt Meats, Etc.   **CHICAGO TENDERLOINS**
Truck Fresh from Farms Daily.   **A SPECIALTY**

The only slaughtering establishment on the Island.

CHARLES ROESCH & SONS

Central Market   Cor. Atlantic and Maryland Aves.
Telephone No. 28.

CITY DRESSED MEATS

Refrigerator Salesrooms,   **Slaughtering Department,**
834, 836, 838 N. Second St., Phila.   Abbatoir Stock Yards, West Phila.

Headquarters for Finest Print Butter
Hotels and Restaurants Supplied   **Rolls and Tenderloins a Specialty**

KESSLER'S ATLANTIC MARKET

No. 1913 Atlantic Avenue

A good supply of all kinds of MEATS, PROVISIONS and VEGETABLES constantly
on hand. Goods delivered free of charge.

MENN'S GIRARD MARKET

2007 Atlantic Avenue

Wholesale and Retail Dealer in Meats and Provisions, Rolls and Tenderloins, Butter,
Eggs and Poultry. Goods delivered.

CHANNELL BROS.

1202 Atlantic Avenue.   Telephone 223

DEALERS IN HIGH GRADE GROCERIES

Specialties: P. E. Sharpless and Darlington Butter. Mocha and Java Coffees. Fine Teas

---

W. R. LEWIS

BUTTER, EGGS AND POULTRY

Telephone 171.   **No. 916 Atlantic Avenue**

F. Stadler's Bakery and Ice Cream Parlor

Corner Atlantic and Virginia Avenues

OPEN ALL THE YEAR   TELEPHONE 99

The Fishing Deck, Strand and Boardwalk

PHYSICIANS.

L. D. BALLIET, M. D.,

HOURS: { 7.30 to 10.00 A. M.
{ 1 to 3 P. M
{ 7 to 9.30 P. M.

HOMOEOPATHIST,

Telephone 63.

1001 Atlantic Avenue.

W. M. BARNES, M. D.,

OFFICE HOURS: { 8 to 10 A. M.
{ 2 to 4 P. M.

17 S. Pennsylvania Avenue.

Long Distance Telephone 265.

DR. G. W. CROSBY.

DR. W. A. CORSON.

DRS. CROSBY AND CORSON,

OFFICE HOURS: { 8 to 10 A. M.
{ 2 to 4 and 7 to 9 P. M.

Telephone 11.

716 Atlantic Avenue.

C. GARRABRANT, M. D.,

Cor. Atlantic and Virginia Aves.

OFFICE HOURS: { Until 10 A. M.
{ 3 to 5 and 7 to 9 P. M.

Medical Offices of the late
DR. WILLARD WRIGHT.

Residence 131 N. Vermont Avenue.   Telephone 63 and 226.

DR. J. ADDISON JOY,

HOURS: { 8 to 9 A. M.
{ 2 to 3.30 P. M.
{ 7 to 8 P. M.

35 S. Illinois Avenue.

MARY MILLER, M. D.,

VENTNOR.

HOURS: { Until 10 A. M.
{ 1 to 3 and 6 to 8 P. M.

Longport Cars pass the door.

127

PHYSICIANS.

DR. B. C. PENNINGTON,

1212 Pacific Avenue.

DR. J. W. SNOWBALL,

HOURS: { To 9 A. M.
{ 1 to 3 P. M.
{ 6 to 7.30 P. M.   Telephone 210.

1519 Pacific Avenue.

DR. WALTER C. SOOY,

HOURS: { 8 to 10 A M.
{ 2 to 4 P. M.
{ 7 to 9 P. M.   Telephone 217

1921 Pacific Avenue.

M. L. SOMERS, M. D.

OFFICE HOURS: { Until 10 A. M.
{ 1 to 3 P. M.
{ 7 to 8 P. M.   Telephone 203.

2012 Pacific Avenue.

J. BART WEBSTER, M. D.

Telephone No. 303.   132 South Maryland Avenue.

M. D. YOUNGMAN, M. D.

1618 Pacific Avenue.

128

DRUGGISTS.

BICKEL'S PHARMACY,

Full line of first-class Drugs,
Perfumery and Toilet Articles.
Prescriptions a Specialty.

Atlantic and Illinois Avenues.

C. J. BROWNLEY,

Successor to M. S. GALBREATH, as Proprietor of

THE GALBREATH APOTHECARY,

New York and Pacific Avenues.

Cushaden DRUGGIST,

Atlantic and Michigan Aves.   Morris Avenue and Boardwalk.

DEAKYNE'S PHARMACY,

A modern store conducted in a
modern way.
" Agency for Walker Gordon Milk."

Pacific Avenue, Corner Kentucky.

JOHN S. INGRAM'S CENTRAL PHARMACY,

New York and Philadelphia Prices.
We sell *lower* than any one in Atlantic City.
Prescriptions called for and delivered to all
parts of the City in shortest time possible.

1408 Atlantic Avenue.

Telephone No. 18.

KEELER'S BEACH PHARMACY,

Kentucky Avenue and Boardwalk,
ATLANTIC CITY.

40th and Locust Streets, Philadelphia.

Ridgway APOTHECARY,

Everything First-Class. Prescriptions a Specialty

Cor. Pennsylvania and Atlantic

Avenues.

Telephone 106.